SKULK

SKULK

A Post-9/11 Comic Novel

Marc Estrin

ProgRESSive

2009

SKULK
A Post 9/11 Comic Novel

Copyright 2008 © by Marc Estrin
All Rights Reserved

Cover design by Delia Robinson,
from a Jerome Lipani idea.

Published by Progressive Press,
PO Box 126, Joshua Tree, Calif. 92252,
www.ProgressivePress.com

ISBN 0-930852-55-9
EAN 978-0930852-55-9
Length: 47,000 words

First Edition
Release December 25, 2008

Table of Contents & Discontents

1. Ho, Ho, Ho.
2. The Wilde Ones.
3. The Kause.
4. Yojimbo.
5. A Radical is a Neocon Who's Been Mugged By Homeland Security.
6. Prairie Fire 1.
7. Santa Unbridled.
8. What Do Kansans Love?
9. The Wheel.
10. She Leaves a Note.
11. Another Trip.
12. Prairie Fire 2.
13. Stalking Santa.
14. The Wich.
15. Job Interview(s).
16. Native American.
17. Dog Days.
18. Modest Doubt is Call'd the Beacon of the Wise.
19. Communiqué #1.
20. Conspiracy Theory.
21. The Angels of the Lord Will Bear You Up.
22. Prairie Fire 3.
23. Liberal, Kansas.
24. Communiqué #2.
25. Frustration.
26. Communiqué #3.
27. And the Fourth Beast Was Like a Flying Eagle.
28. The Last Interview.
29. Windhovers.
30. All the News that's Fit to Print.

ONE

Ho, Ho, Ho

"So who is this guy in the red suit? Who is this old man sitting innocent little children serially on his lap, murmuring to them "What would you like? What would you really like?", smiling, and taking pictures?

"Who is this guy anyway? What's his <u>real</u> name? Klaus? Nicholas? Mikolas? Père Noel? A.k.a Babbo Natale? A.k.a Hotei-osho? A.k.a Kanakaloka? He is everywhere, the global hegemon of Christmas.

"What is his name? Santa. The holy one."

Teresa Lee Skulkington, of the Connecticut Skulkingtons, last of the Glickman Series lecturers, stood beside the lectern at Wichita State University's Wilner Auditorium, the better to show off her slinky red dress, and herself inside it. T.L., she was called, as in Tough Love. She will be called something else soon enough.

"I won't begin to detail the psychological damage this figure creates: the life-long suspicion that parents — and all authority figures — lie; the consequent loss of trust in the world and its mythical heroes; the cynical understanding that it's best not to question, especially those things from which we might profit; the existential gloom that engulfs us when we discover that the world is not the loving, caring place we once thought it was.

"Instead, tonight, I want to interrogate the belief system of you liberals out there, all you college progressives, you good little girls and boys who will soon have your high five-figure jobs, and your white picket fence to guard your 2.4 children."

Good-humored hissing in the auditorium, largely — but not entirely — from the sign-laden protesters in the back. From them, the first one and a half repetitions of a chant: T-L, T-L, WE DON'T LIKE YOU VERY WELL!

"Yes, yes. Typical liberal embrace of freedom of speech. Freedom for those in the back, but not for me. No matter how loony, sick, grotesque, stupid, corrupt, anti-family, or traitorous your ideas are, dear gas-bags, bed-wetters, and human Gumbys out there, they will always be faithfully broadcast by the liberal media, which will do all it can to shut out all other views. Like my interrogating your liberal myth of Santa Claus. So just shut up. I'm getting paid big bucks to be here – courtesy, by the way of your Clare Booth Luce Society, yay, – so since I, at least, want to <u>earn</u> my keep, I'm going to go ahead anyway, whether you like it or not."

Applause and boos.

"This is one bang-up woman," thought Richard Gronsky, behind his social-comment nose-glasses which functioned also as a poor disguise. He was one of the more popular assistant professors in the history department. "I mean she is a looker, even better than her book covers. Check those muscular arms, those lovely calves. Hard bod, for sure." Even history professors have fantasies.

"Perhaps I should define the term liberal?," the speaker continued. "Liberals. You know, the fuzzy-minded blue-state minority who thinks AIDS is spread by a lack of federal funding, or that guns in the hands of red-blooded Americans are more dangerous than weapons of mass destruction in the hands of the ragheads..."

Serious cat-calls this time from the right-thinking left.

"OK, OK...I obviously don't need to define 'liberal' for you, as you seem to have mastered the subject. So let's go right to Santa Baby."

Here she pulled out from behind the lectern a red satin, ermine-trimmed stocking cap, and placed it coquettishly on her silky blond head. Out in the fourth row, Dr. Gronsky thought he'd seen such a face before. *Playboy* perhaps – or was it *Playgirl?* Perhaps it was only the pom-pom. In any case, politically incorrect or not, the audience did seem ready to be entertained. Hey – it was a free event at the end of the semester.

"Because you are all – mostly all — sheep who need linear leading by the nose, I shall take you alphabetically through some of Santa's major characteristics and abuses, each of which, of course, <u>should</u> be roundly rejected by liberals – if they weren't the weasely hypocrites that they are. And remember, when you see a house with a red plastic Santa lit up outside, with twinkle-light reindeer feeding in the front yard snow, <u>that</u> is the house of a liberal. There are many in Wichita. When you see a creche with an infant Christ, that is <u>not</u> the home of a liberal. That is the home of a Christian. Of them in Wichita there are even more.

"Let's start at A with animal rights. How can you liberals so enthusiastically endorse such cruelty to reindeer? It is very difficult, not to say dangerous, for reindeer to land on a roof, especially the sloped ones so common out on the plains. Where is your ASPCA on this? Where, for that matter, is air traffic control? How many dead and crippled reindeer go unreported in the liberal press? And the fur trim on Santa's suit? Where is PETA? Why isn't every Santa — department store and real – attacked with spray paint blood on their trim. Why isn't Pamela Anderson displaying her lettuce leaf bikini as an ethical alternative? Hypocrisy. Pure liberal hypocrisy."

Richard was in ecstasy. Here was a maniac after his own heart. A bit right-wing, to be sure, but a true fanatical droll.

"C. Class issues. Who subsidizes Santa? Who writes the checks? The well-to-do. The rich. The richer the better. The poor are left scrounging for Santa's toys among the cracked and spittled rejects at the Salvation army – and feeling guilty about it, full of envy and resentment that Santa's fallout in the material world should be based on ability to pay. Could it be that you liberals <u>want</u> class war – as long as you can stay above the fray in your gated communities and athletic clubs?

"But what are you doing supporting the satanic duo of commercialism and consumerism? Liberals are supposed to hate that stuff – the media-induced gluttonous craving for material goods. Have you ever listened in on what the kids are asking for on the lap of the red-suited God? It ain't hay. There are, of course those liberal moppets brain-washed enough to sputter out "I want world peace" to a disgusted controller of the means of production. They leave that scarlet lap hating their martinet parents until such time as they are amply rewarded with all the goodies they would have listed if they were honest. Excellent liberal training in talking the talk, but riding the walk in their little electric car with batteries provided. And thus capitalism continues its merry dance with liberals playing the tune. See, little Virginia? There <u>is</u> a free lunch."

Richard was plotting already. How would he detain her? How get her away from her host, whoever they might be? The Yale Review, Yale Law School, it said in the program. With looks like that, she's probably heard it all. There would be a reception somewhere. He'd find out where. He was, after all, on the faculty.

"D. Diversity. Basically a white, penis-people operation. (*Applause from Richard's nemesis, the racially diverse WU Herstory Society.*) All the elves are white. Hold up your hands if you've seen any other kind depicted. (*Not a hand raised.*) And except for the big boss, short, all short. Shorter than he. Principle of hiring? Size-ism? What about tall-people rights? Ex-basketball players? Are tall elves 'vertically challenged'? If so, are they protected by the Americans with Disabilities Act? Or doesn't that count if they're not American? Are liberals not concerned? What's with you?

"E. A liberal favorite: ecology. Can you imagine the environmental impact of a major manufacturing operation on the fragile tundra, the global warming effect on the glaciers? I'm sure Santa's factory burns tons of fossil fuels – that isn't all hand work – at that scale it can't be – and where, my friends, are the ozone holes? As your Marxist Frankfurt School friends love to say, "That is no coincidence."

Richard was bowled over and a half. His PhD. had been on "The Conception of Freedom in the Early Frankfurt School." He <u>had</u> to meet this woman, who continued her alphabetical exegesis.

"And E," she hammered home, "for no less a threatened species than epistemology. "Won't Santa get burned if he comes down the chimney?" Or, "How can he come down the chimney if we don't have a fireplace?" Or even "How can reindeer fly if they don't have wings?" Think of the answers liberals give their children – those charming tots they're already grooming for Harvard. All questions discouraged, or declared irrelevant by fiat. Liberals are supposed to be interested in developing a questioning mind. Like really?

And what about GLBT issues – that's pronounced 'glbt'? All those songs that rhyme 'Christmas toys' with 'girls and boys'.

The kids in Girl and Boyland
will have a jubilee...' she sang, and sweetly.
Will there be nothing for the RU12? set?"
(More cheers from the Herstorians.)

Richard's heart was doing an Elvin Jones riff. Calm down, old man. She's just a typical, if leading, example of the new conservative star-babe. I mean you can't really put Karl Rove out there and expect young voters to salute. What will be, will be. If we're meant to meet, we will. But with some alternate grooming, she could sure be dynamite for the cause. The Kause.

"Health," T.L. continued. "This man is fat. Fat, fat, fat. Is fat what you liberals want to model for your children? He smokes like a chimney. Maybe he doesn't inhale. (*Sniggers from those old enough to remember a previous president.*) But if it weren't so cold up there, metastasis would be in the saddle, with second-hand smoke for the elves and Mrs. Santa and the reindeer. What are the cancer rates? No one is saying. Cardiovascular morbidity and mortality? Maybe that's why the elves are short.

"And L for labor. My god, I wouldn't be surprised to find a detachment of Pinkertons up there. Is Santa paying for health care? Are there other bennies? If so, you never hear about them. Or about elves on strike. Do they even have a union? If not, why not? When does the workshop become a sweatshop, even in the arctic? When does it cross the line into oppression? Liberals, are you listening, or doesn't it really matter?

"I needn't even get into P-for-privacy issues, with lists and checks and video surveillance. He sees you when you're sleeping – That's S. S.S."

Richard pulled out his digital recorder. Though he had come, like many others, to scoff, he remained now, if not exactly to pray, then perhaps to prey. No wedding ring? He wanted this woman. He wanted her mental and physical musculature on his side, not on theirs. He wanted her voice in his little box to remind him, should it be necessary, that he wanted her entirety.

"Taxes? You liberals like taxes. Hey, this guy is giving stuff away. So where's the sales tax on equivalent value, the gift tax? No paper trail for audit. Very clever. A semi-faith-based 501-c-3. Liberals, do you smell fraud? If not, why not?

"Trade policy. Liberals, this guy is a total free marketeer. Anathema, anathema. He crosses international borders with impunity — without a passport. No luggage inspection, no body search, no checking his laptop. Hey, is he really fat? Are there explosives in there? How does he get away with this stuff? Call out the Social Forum!

"And you know what makes up 75% of what's in those uninspected sacks? W-for-War toys! Shoot up the Ragheads games. (*Ambiguous hissing.*) So where's the anti-gun lobby? Where is the peacenik chorus condemning the plague of small arms? Cat got your tongues?

"And last but not least, W-for-Women's issues. Beyond all those gender-stereotypic toys, are you libbers not interested in

Mrs. Santa? No butch or grrrrlll she. Stay-at-home support for her tubbie-hubbie? And where are their children? Is Mrs. Santa um, pro-choice? Have there been any 'procedures' in the back room? And where are the female elves? Also staying home? Why? Is Mrs. Santa just a front for some hankypank with those sweet little worker elves?

"All you liberals and progressives out there, I want to see some gumption. I want to see some progress. Rewrite all those picket signs. SMASH SANTA-ISM. No, better, direct action. I want to see you out there burning all those big plastic Santas – no, wait, that'd make pollution. So just collect them from people's yards and trash 'em – except that's really bad for the landfills. Well, libs, you've got a problem. That, children, is the mess you get when you keep Christ out of Christmas.

"Season's greetings, ho ho ho, and have a merry — um, winter break."

Richard watched her walk majestically through the door, stage right.

TWO

The Wilde Ones

Richard Gronsky, it must be said, was a hunk. At forty, very, very athletic and handsome. It was a mainstay of his academic popularity.

He had the kind of good looks attractive to both sexes: the young men in his classes saw in him an easy-going manly beauty, almost classical, yet so unconcerned-with-self as to radiate some essential malehood. Perhaps the good-humored, active father they'd love to have had. He was, in an innocent way, beyond them, off somewhere else. He'd never never think of competition. And so neither would they.

For the young women – well, it doesn't need saying. Except that while stirring their juices, he also put out enough devoted-young-scholar vibes to make them feel almost safe when alone with him in his office. Students, for him, were out-of-bounds.

His colleagues loved his sweet insouciance. At least a score had adopted his nose-glasses in a kind of peripatetic Marxian sodality, showing up singly or in force at appropriate events, including important faculty meetings. What could the administrators do except laugh to demonstrate their cool? Still, the nose-glasses presence hung in the air throughout, with exceptional, and often salubrious, effect.

Single women academics felt most vulnerable, and not far behind them, young husbands or husbands of the young. But his track record was so sterling as to turn his very power – so unutilized — into a badge of virtue. Confidence. Amazing. I can take this guy home without bringing on trouble. True, there were women and men who hid their longing, but for these such hiding was common enough, and longstanding.

It was thus with some confidence that Richard Gronsky – nose glasses in pocket — jumped onstage, and followed T.L.'s groupies out the stage right door, and up to the reception at the

Student Center gallery. The picketers were there too, polite Kansans with their polite signs, taking political revenge by snarfing down the shrimp and egg rolls before the conservative majority could get to them.

Richard was all in black. Black turtleneck, edgy-faculty-retro-existential, black Levis, and motorcycle boots. This was not "costume", but strictly pragmatic: it was cold out there on the motorcycle. In the gallery warmth, he carried his black leather jacket over his shoulder, while nursing his Guinness, Dedalus-like, with the other hand. He watched and waited for his moment.

T.L. Skulkington, red and shimmery, was working the room while the room worked her. The red and the black they were, military and church, still separate.

And then they stood together at his BSA in the parking lot. A simple "Would you like to go for a motorcycle ride?" doesn't work with every girl on a Kansas November night, but this was a girl who couldn't say no – to any implied challenge to her macho supremacy.

"What's BSA?" she asked, looking at the logo sunburst on the fuel tank. "Bullshit Alliance?"

"Red and gold, like you," he said. It wasn't a line. She *was* red and gold, like a proper princess. "Birmingham Small Arms. Out of business in '72. This is a '70 Thunderbolt classic. I do my own maintenance."

Somehow, she was not impressed.

"The Brits can't build engines," she pontificated. Someone once had told her that.

"Well, then you'll be all the more delighted with the ride."

"Sidesaddle? This dress is not made for spreading the legs, as it were."

"It handles better if you spread your legs, as it were. Here are some pants, and a warmer jacket."

He reached into the saddlebag, and pulled out a second outfit much like his own.

"These are kind of big, wouldn't you say?"

"Hey, beggars can't be choosers, you know? I mean guests."

She hiked her dress up over her hips, (nice calves, nice thighs) put on the leather pants, and squirmed the dress back over elephantine legs.

"That won't get you far in the leg-spreading department," he noted.

"Damn!" she said, more humiliated than flustered.

And reaching down, mid-thigh, she peeled the Lycra up over her hips, her body and head, and stood there in bra, necklace, and earrings, shivering.

"Nice?" she asked. "And I only just met you. Now how about that jacket, buddy?"

Was it that he wanted to look a little longer, or that he felt she should know what he was giving her to wear? He took a moment to turn the coat to demonstrate its emblem.

"Wilde Won," she read. "Very clever. Now hand it over before I hypotherm."

In went her arms, as he held it out, gentlemanly.

"Whooooa!" she inhaled. "Leather ain't flannel," she observed.

"You'll warm up in a minute."

He primed the gas, and kick-started the engine to a British version of a purr. She deposited the red dress with the red coat in the saddle bag, and hopped on behind him.

"Put on the helmet," he said. His own was already on.

"I want my golden hair to stream in the wind. It's why I accepted your invite."

"Illegal in Kansas. Mandatory helmet law."

"Fucking government!" she murmured, spread the helmet, and buckled in.

She pushed back against him. This was the first chance she'd had to really read his jacket. In a circle, WILDE WON, H.M. PRISON, READING. Within the circle, a shaven-bald Wilde, looking strangely like an acromegalic skull. She poked a finger into Wilde's left eye.

"Is this what I've got on my back?" she wanted to know.

"Yes. We are presently the only two members of the Wilde Won, M.C."

"But he didn't win. He got thrown into prison for ass-fucking, and died a couple of years after he got out, broke."

"Meningitis, T.L.. Could happen to any of us."

"So how can you say he won?"

"Let's go for a ride, and I'll tell you."

Vroom, vroom, off they went, 0-60 in 10.4 seconds once out of the lot. She'd never say so, but she loved it. It was her virgin ride. Under the leather of his back, she sensed a sacred beast.

"Where are we going?" she screamed into his helmet.

"Up to the Speedway," he screamed back. "Then you'll see what this British thing can really do."

"I don't want to. I've seen it already. I want to know why you think Wilde won. As long as I'm wearing his jacket."

"I was only kidding. We're going to the country club, the golf course. You do country clubs, I hear."

"Oh yeah? Who'd you hear from?"

"I read Brock's book."

"Motherfucker traitor! Don't believe a word he says."

"OK. Then we can go to the Speedway."

"No. The country club. 11PM in mid-November is no season for speedways."

When they stopped for gas, she practiced her wilde-ness by stealing a Mounds bar from the convenience store.

Vroom, vroom again, and then it was quiet.

The Wichita Country Club is built beside a world-class golf course of lush fairways and tranquil ponds and streams. Extensive paths are good for jogging by the hoi polloi, and highly recommended for business deals and romantic walks. This night it was gray and misty, the sky heavy with vapor, and backlit by the moon in fantastic, spectral shapes. They made their way past the clubhouse towards hole 7, with its narrow fairway in a copse of trees. The red and the black had become the black and the black in this, Nature's manicured gothic. They sat against the trees, and watched the sky. All armies seemed at rest.

"So what's with Wilde?" she asked.

"Ever read 'The Soul of Man Under Socialism'?"

"In case you haven't guessed, I'm no great fan of socialism."

"This is Wildean socialism. No Marx, no Lenin, no Trotsky, no Stalin."

"I'm not sure I'd want Oscar Wilde as Commissar of Truth."

"You might. He's a forerunner of Ayn Rand."

"Now you're getting warmer."

"He's big on Individualism."

"So am I. But I'm cold," she said.

"Come over here."

She left her tree, and snuggled back against his chest. He held her around her chest and haaaaaa-d her ears with gentle breath.

"I've never had my ears warmed. Cut it out."

"I feel responsible for their being cold."

"I'll deal. Individualism."

"For Wilde, that's the whole point of living: find thyself, be thyself."

"OK. Where's the socialism?"

"He thought the need to do shit work keeps people from developing themselves. And that private property creates a restrictive puny individualism — demoralizing with its endless protection, insurance, and maintenance. Gain, not personal growth becomes the main thing."

"Keep your arms off my tits."

"Sorry. I got carried away. That is, not with your tits."

"Why not with my tits? What's wrong with my tits?"

"Uh... nothing. I mean... "

"So we're not supposed to own anything?"

"Nothing that can be stolen. That's the test. Real riches can't be stolen."

"So who cleans up the shit?"

"Machines are there to do the shitwork. The state will be there to make what is useful; but humans are there to make what is beautiful."

"Utopian slop."

"One of the great sentences in the piece — I have it pasted up over my desk — is 'A map of the world that does not include

Utopia is not worth even glancing at, for it leaves out the one country at which Humanity is always landing.'"

"I'm sitting here between your legs, and you've got your hands on my tits... "

"I don't."

"Well, you could if you wanted to."

"I... "

"... and you are laying it on thick about Utopia? This doesn't even sound like conversation. And I'm still cold. I want to go back to the guest house."

They walked back to the bike.

"So you're not going to join my Utopia?" Richard asked.

"Are you kidding? What utopia? Where?"

"Here. In the free state of Kansas. After we secede."

"My mother told me to stay away from maniacs."

"All right. I won't tell you about the plan. The Kause with a K."

"K for Kafka. Take me home."

En route T.L. Skulkington, of the Connecticut Skulkingtons, sang out "Candyman" to the deserted streets. And home they went to terse goodnights.

THREE

The Kause

After a short theogeographic preamble, the Kansas State Constitution enumerates twenty points of a bill of Kansan rights. Two of these were of particular interest to Dr. Richard Gronsky of the WSU history faculty, the chairperson, treasurer, secretary and only member of the Free Kansas Party:

> *Sec. 2. All political power is inherent in the people, and all free governments are founded on their authority, and are instituted for their equal protection and benefit. No special privileges or immunities shall ever be granted by the legislature, which may not be altered, revoked or repealed...*

> *Sec. 20. This enumeration of rights shall not be construed to impair or deny others retained by the people; and all powers not herein delegated remain with the people.*

The implication was clear: Kansas could legally, and in good conscience, nay, excellent — the best of conscience — secede from the United States of America, should that be the will of its citizens.

But at the moment, he had no one to whom to give the secret salute (two fingers up, thumb at their base — the American Sign sign for "K") Perhaps the Kause's low membership was <u>because</u> of the letter K: Kafka and Joseph K being no one's version of dessert. Then there was the KKK of course, and its macaronic epigones, Amerika, Amerikkka. But then again there was Kwik-stop and K-mart and the Keystone Kops. No one seemed to object to them. It must be something else.

GRONSKY

It's false consciousness, that what it is! People don't understand what's going on in the world. They vote against their own interests. They...

KARL

Nein, Richard, you haf it backwarts. The real problems of Men stem from contradictions in the reality world. As long as people's activities cannot fix the contradictions, they project them into their ideas. Their consciousness is not false: it shows <u>realistically</u> the structures of the wrong-built world. But ve must not only interpret for them the world: the point is to change it. Jah, jah.

GRONSKY

OK. Good. Gut. Change it, change it. Kansas can be a free territory again, no more contradictions. Kansas — a free territory of the mind.

So that's the way he went. A secession movement. Why not? It was time. It had precedent. The Kansas-Nebraska Act. States' rights. Articles 2 and 20.

A Declaration of Independence by the People of the
Free State of Kansas
in Wichita, July 4th, 2004
(drafted by Richard R. Gronsky, Wichita State University)

When, in the course of human events, it becomes necessary for one people to dissolve the political bands which have connected them with another, etc., etc., *let them declare the causes which impel them to the separation.*

Jefferson wouldn't mind, he thought.

We hold these truths to be self-evident, that all men are created equal, and are endowed with certain unalienable Rights, that among these are Life, Liberty and the pursuit of Happiness. — *That to secure these rights,* etc., etc. all that stuff still relevant, and down to

Let the reasons for Kansas independence be submitted to a candid world..."

It's a long document, the Gronsky declaration, and not hard to imagine: a standard litany of left-wing complaints about big business taking over, about big agriculture forcing farmers off their lands, about a government big enough for guns, but not for butter.

GRONSKY

What do you mean, "the standard litany"? These are people's lives, their cares, their griefs, their stinging tears and destruction. If that's... standard — all the more reason to shout it out: Fuck you. "Standard."

MARC

I was going to say that the declaration was infused with his fascinating sense of history, of Bleeding Kansas, new and old, of border ruffians and war, of John Brown's prophetic path, culminating a vision of future history consistent with the triumph of freedom. Is that better?

GRONSKY

Yes.

MARC

He wrote persuasively that the United States was no longer politically, economically, agriculturally, environmentally, socially, morally or culturally sustainable, and that the larger society was dragging Kansas down with it.

GRONSKY

And so it is.

MARC

That's what I said, so stop giving me a hard time. And that the Kansas heartland, even with every missile silo emptied, still runs the risk of attack by its association with the unprovoked, unilateral and "preemptive" attacks on nations with which the US disagrees.

GRONSKY

Don't forget, we Kansans also pay out a lot more than we get back from the Feds.

MARC

Yes. That, too.

There was a moral, legal, and absolute imperative, he wrote, for an independent-minded Kansas to revert back to its historically superior status as the Free-State Territory it was between 1854 and 1861.

"This is a call for Kansans to reclaim their souls, and demonstrate an alternative to a nation obsessed with money, power, size, speed and greed. Let us secure our future with the skills and strengths of our past, our ingenuity and our self-reliance."

He had, believe it or not, created this document not on his word processor, but by writing it out longhand using the mother-of-pearl Waterman he'd gotten from Uncle Irving for his Bar Mitzvah. Somehow it felt more politically — or at least historically — correct. But for the final paragraph, driven by the same befuddled urge, he thought he'd reach farther back — even unto quilldom.

But where to get a quill? Where did <u>they</u> get quills? Why didn't a historian know where to get a quill? Stop the presses! Out to the quad. Pigeons, where were they when you needed them? He actually did find a pigeon feather — maybe it was a pigeon feather — but it was less than two inches long, and better used to tickle someone's nose than to sign a historic manifesto.

GRONSKY

I know — Ben Franklin. I'll go to Ben Franklin. They must have quills — old Ben used quills. Or they'll have feathers, bigger than this one anyway. It's a crafts store. This is a craft.

Down he roared on his BSA to the Ben Franklin out on Central. Would they have feathers big enough for quills? He'd never held out the wing of any large, dead bird to select the best and longest feathers. Growing up in New York City, he'd never even seen a large dead bird. As far as he knew geese or turkeys didn't even <u>live</u> in New York. At least with their feathers on. Grabbing the best feathers may have been good for Thomas Jefferson, with his own goose flock, or turkeys just for his quills, but for me, he thought, they'd better be at Ben Franklin.

Into the store, asthmatogenic smell.

"Do you have feathers? Like for quills? Quill pens?"

"We have bags of 'Indian Feathers'. Aisle five at the rear, right, near the top."

Six feathers for a buck and a quarter. Made in Taiwan. Chinese Indians, why not? Half the tubes crushed. Better buy two bags. Three.

Chinese Indian Feathers in California saddlebags on British Machine zoomed back to Gronsky's apartment in Old Town Wichita. He dipped his first Indian feather in ink, but it just shed the liquid like water off a ...you know. Think, Richard. What would Ben Franklin do?

I need a razor blade.

Damn!

Out the door again to the Rexall's down the block. Maybe he should get an Xacto knife like he had as a kid. They didn't have any. No single-edge blades either. Back to Ben Franklin? No. He'd just cut his fingers off with a double-edged Gillette.

Back in the apartment, the Waterman on display under the desk lamp, the Indian feather looking nothing like it. Even in principle. Where, for instance were its gills?

But he had fifteen feathers minus six to experiment with. And he was a historian. So how about a diagonal cut across the cylinder to begin. Oooo, lots of ...stuff... inside, membranes and like that. Got to get all that out. Maybe I don't need all this feathery stuff on the feather. It's just getting in the way. Give it a little hair cut up the spine here. Doesn't look much like those ostrichy plume things you see in the movies, but there are probably not that many ostriches wandering around Germany in the middle ages. Wait a minute. A pen knife! I've got a pen knife. Why is it called a pen knife if not to? Somewhere in this drawer. Ah.

Six Indian feathers later, with three extra just in case, Prof. Richard R. Gronsky dipped a quill-like pen into a bottle of Parker Blue-Black ink – and it held. And it made marks on paper. Sort of. You wouldn't want to do interlinear annotations, or even fill out a crossword puzzle with it, but it was a pen that wrote. So he sat down to write the first of three more drafts of the final paragraph. The spatters were authentic:

"Therefore, we, the sovereign people of the state of Kansas, do hereby declare our independence from the United States of America, and call upon the Kansas Legislature to authorize a convention of the people to vote on rescinding the petition for statehood approved by the Kansas Assembly in July, 1859 and ratified by the US Congress on January 29th, 1861."

And with a flourish worthy of John Hancock, he signed his name (without his academic title) at the bottom of the document, dipped the pen again, and filled in the "...sky" which had run out of ink the first time, but was now emphatically new, so that his signature struck the reader as quite like Gron<u>sky</u>, or given his half-print, half-script, GronSKY. Plus some black suns spattered. Yes, why not, he thought. Free the enslaved mind. The sky's the limit.

And as if to underline that potential, there was at that moment, at the very moment of the flourish, the quill poised dripping in the air, like a hairy head in the hand of the Demon Barber, at that very moment, there was a sharp rapping at the door, and before Richard could lay down his pen, the door was impatiently tried, and flung open — and in she walked.

"Hi, honey, I'm home."

It was T.L. — and who else could it be? T.L., and none other.

"Wha..?"

She lugged two large Louis Vuitton suitcases in from the hallway. He ran to help — too late. The Armanis were inside the door, and she had plopped down on the sofa.

"What are you doing here?"

"I've got a Kansas project, and you're going to help me."

"But why me? I... "

"We'll need a motorcycle for getting around, and the Ladies Auxiliary Speaker's Bureau doesn't have one. Besides, I don't know anyone else with an apartment in downtown Wichita. Should I leave?"

"No, but... "

"No buts. You have to be committed. I know that's hard for a liberal. But with me, it's all or nothing. Is it all or nothing with you?" she sang.

"Well, sure, but... "

"Which?"

"Which what?"

"All — or nothing?"

"Isn't that a little extreme?" he asked.

"Like you're with us or against us?" Her question for his.

"Exactly."

"Well then, are you with us or against us?"

"Who's 'us'?" he wanted to know.

"Me. For or against?"

"I'm for you, but... "

"No buts."

"OK. For."

"That's better. But first, time for bed."

She grabbed him by the hand.

"Where's the bedroom?"

"In there. It's only three thirty. It's still light out."

"I'm jet-lagged."

"But it's only an hour difference. Were you in New York?"

"I was up late. Time for bed."

What could he do?

Afterwards, they lay in bed, smoking. Just like in the movies. Sixties movies anyway: the room was full of the sweet smell of Bethesda Gold Plus.

"I have this friend, who shall go unnamed," she said, who works at NSF. He's part of the Heritage Foundation Caucus over there. The heritage in question is this vial of actual seeds from George Washington's hemp plantation which he says has been passed down from generation to generation by the Sons of Liberty. What do I know? Anyway, they're doing a hybrid of Heritage and NSF by creating a genetically modified plant, *Cannabis sativa* plus *Ginko biloba*. It's got pot content plus — THC 18-20% — in the shape of a small ginko tree. It opens the cerebral circulation at the same time as it turns it on... "

"Yeah, I noticed. I thought it was you."

"It is — with a little help from my friends. And the cops have no clue. You can grow a jungle full of them on your front lawn, they'd never know."

"But how did you get this stuff through security?"

"In my Maidenform bra, how else?"

She reached down and grabbed it from the floor on her side of the bed.

"See?"

She pushed and poked one out. In the sewn channel where the underwires had been ran a tightly packed chain of tightly rolled joints.

"Neat, huh? They don't show up on x-ray, they don't set off metal detectors, the dogs are confused by the perfume, and the human animals would never feel me up to check. If they did, they'd be sorry."

"You would think they'd be smart enough to... "

"Smart enough? Minimum wage government morons? The ones who ask you phenomenally asinine questions like 'Has anybody but you packed your bags, m'am?' 'Why yes, Sir, they were packed by the bomb service back at headquarters.' Are you kidding? These are the cretins who are still instructing you how to buckle your seat belt."

"The NLF used to carry millet in little cloth tubes like this," Richard informed her, " — like necklaces. They won the war on millet."

"They didn't win the war," she corrected him. "<u>We</u> won the war. Ho-Ho-Ho-Chi-Minh City is now as capitalist as Hong Kong. They're drinking Coke and eating Macdonalds and downloading rap on their iPods. They vote with us in your beloved UN. We have trade agreements. They all speak English. And we haven't paid them a cent of reparations. But I suppose you think the peace movement won the war."

Richard thought it best to let this go. MJ *biloba + orgasmus in excelcis* had decreased his instinct for argument. She, on the other hand... But perhaps she had a higher tolerance.

"I'm glad you've come," he said.

"I came three times, if you really want to know."

"I mean come here — to visit."

"I came here to work," she insisted. "That righteous prig isn't going to get away with this."

"Who, what?"

"Didn't I tell you? I'm out after Tommy Frank's ass."

"Tommy Frank the general?"

"No, Tommy Frank, the dickhead. Thomas Frank. Of the liberal pundit blabocracy. Chicago. *The Baffler*. The Barney Frank for intellectuals. And on the Commie New York Times best-seller list for four months."

"What is?"

"You haven't read *What's The Matter With Kansas*??"

"Oh yeah. I mean no. I read reviews."

"You can read the copy in my bag."

"What's got your goat?"

"Oh, nothing. Just his attacks on everything I and other real Americans hold dear. Like reverence, courtesy, kindness, cheerfulness, loyalty, hard work. You know, the benighted behavior of the down-home working stiffs in the red states. I'm out here to write an anti-book. I'm going to show up each and everything Frank says as the elitist, slanderous bullshit it is. You and I are going to drive around on your BSA and interview hundreds of Kansans. We're going to Pizza Huts and White Castles and Applebees, Cargill and Cessna and Raytheon, we're going to explore the loyal, patriotic hearts of Frank's bumpkins, the pain which Clinton and even Bush didn't feel, we're going to see that their voting behavior is not paradoxical, that it doesn't reflect false consciousness as you mandarin Marxists love to think, that it not only responds accurately to what the <u>liberals</u> have put them through, but it represents an unstoppable wave for healing America, and beyond that, the world. That's what we're going to do. I hope you have snow tires on that thing."

This was not, perhaps, a marriage made in heaven. But then it was not yet a marriage at all. At this point it wasn't even a particularly civil union. But the sex was great.

Here's the long and short of it: When little Richie Gronsky was a kid, his mother read him *Goodnight Moon*, and later *Ferdinand the Bull* for a bedtime story. When T.L. Skulkington of the Connecticut Skulkingtons was still little Terry S., her father read her *1984* and *The Fountainhead*. Every time they went out together for ice cream, Lawrence Charles Skulkington, the corporate lawyer, would take bites out of his little daughter's ice cream cone — "This is for sales tax... this is for income tax... this is for social security tax... this is for estate tax... this is for excess profits tax..." — until the poor little girl was whetting her teeth in her held-back tears. Richie, on the other hand, got an eclair or a Mounds bar — whole ones — anytime he wanted one. When Terry became Teresa, her father died of a heart attack. When Richie became Richard, his mother died of breast cancer. It all equals out in the end. But in the middle of the beginning, the differences intrigue.

His pentagon was Broch, Kierkegaard, Illich, Chomsky, and McCartney; hers, de Maistre, Burke, Rand, Strauss, and Garcia. The overlap, to wit, was small. He did, he convinced her, he did understand the famous "red state 'values'". But in this context: that we are living in an epoch of extreme disorientation, in the dominion of death, the confusion of our decline commingled with the confusion of our quest. She agreed. It was the liberals' fault.

But from whence, he asked, came the enthusiasm for war and slaughter? The isolation of value-systems! "Business is business," say the businessmen; "This is war" says the military; "L'art pour l'art" say the artists; "All's fair in love" say the starry-eyed — a vast cacophony of single-value systems, each thrown back on itself, separate from any other, claiming equality — nay, superiority — of purpose and method, each intent on the ruthless pursuit of its own goals, each excluding and overwhelming all others. This anarchy of value-systems was the recipe for the radical evil of our time. OK. She listened.

And the more comprehensive a value-system was, the greater its goals, then the greater the chance that evil lay <u>within</u> it, innate, non-excludable. But when systems are disconnected, each seeing itself as a totality, blindly inflated toward the infinite, all evil within them becomes radical. Human actors feel "rational" even when their effect is highly irrational, totally nuts. Words and comparisons lose their meaning, all values collapse, and what is left is naked action, violence, gangster methods, an overriding faith in murder. People become ethically depraved. She listened warily, without entirely disagreeing. It explained, for instance, Bill Clinton.

Her stance was not without love — tough and sometimes tender. His despair was not without hope — sometimes hope for the present, but often hope for the end. His softness could be hardhearted; her hardness concealed some soft. They agreed on the need for a leap from this thick-willed world, ecstatic for security, to some other. Wilde's essay was, in fact, the triangulation between them, as she admitted after reading it. In the freedom of his imagined society of artists, they could sense a model of freedom for all. If Gronsky could endure the individualism, T.L. would put up with the socialism.

The Free State of Kansas could be their common cause. And it turned out they both hated the same people — liberals — he from the left, she from the right. "Hatred stirreth up strifes," says Proverbs, but in this case, it made them a team — Gronsky and Skulkington. Or was it Skulkington and Gronsky?

A feminist might have argued for the latter. But T.L. was anti-feminism. On the other hand, her ego might support it anyway. He argued that G&S was a prized abbreviation, twisted here to freshness. She offered that S&G were the value stamps of her childhood, and that even her rich parents saved books of them. He countered that it was S&H Green Stamps, not S&G. He was right. She thought "Skulkington & Gronsky" had a nice feminine ending he of all people should appreciate, but it turned out that he valued the strong Beethovenian cadence of "Gronsky & Skulk" with the "ington" muttered arhythmically under the breath. They left it, like Schrödinger's cat, in a state of superposition.

He did mention at their next post-coital smoke-in that her vial of George Washington's ginko reminded him of John Brown.

"Um?" she said between her teeth. "How so?" She passed him the joint.

"Before Harper's Ferry, he sent six men on a mission to capture some relative of George's who owned a sword and pistol of George's. Free the guy's slaves, and bring him back – that was the assignment - and especially bring back that sword and the pistol. Pistol came originally from Lafayette and the sword from Frederick the Great." He handed her the roach.

"He's from Kansas or something... ?"

"Frederick the Great?"

"No, idiot. John Brown."

"He lived here. Not far. Osawatomie."

"Let's go there."

Yes, and the sex was also good — I mean great.

FOUR

Yojimbo

Kaufmann's Department Store occupied the lower six floors of the second highest skyscraper in Wichita, a 14-story building of classic plains design with a richly-ornamented, dark-red brick façade and vaulted, twelve-columned ground floor. Originally conceived as emporium *cum* city-center, that cathedral-like space contained an ornate dais at one end from which the story — probably apocryphal — was that Vladimir Horowitz had once played a piano recital in the late thirties. Why Horowitz should be tooling around Kansas at the time is unclear. Perhaps it was some WPA New Deal stunt. The deal on the dais these days was not Horowitz, but Santa, reigning on his throne in most inappropriate splendor.

Richard Gronsky went on and on with his new pal about how the workshop economy of the north pole had evolved into hierarchical domination of the means of production by a new ruling class — as exemplified by the white-bearded Uncle Fatso up there on stage, expropriating surplus credit for the sweatshop labor of his faceless minions. He likened the throne and red garments to that of the Pope, and the altar-effect to the bourgeois deification of commerce. She liked this. Perhaps the handsome pig might see the anti-liberal light after all. She <u>did</u> like the Pope, and commerce, and hierarchy — but for the moment, she would let that go. She was there to buy a Christmas present for Dad.

In the place of a store directory, Kaufmann's used Santa's stage as a setting for a clamoring tableau vivant-mort, a curved, forty-foot diorama of typical merchandise selections arranged left to right by floors — perfume & makeup, jewelry, bags & accessories, shoes, juniors, women, sportswear, outerwear, men's wear, lingerie, maternity, children's wear, gifts, bridal & formal, domestics, furniture, small appliances... In their midst sat Santa, and snaking to the foot of the stage, a line of children with their camera-toting parents, the children for the most part embarrassed or quaking with fear, the parents coaching them as if for their first dissertation defense. Richard took it all in, in a spirit both critical and forgiving, while Teresa surveyed the dioramic choices.

"Hmm. Jewelry Dad has up the gazoo. Sportswear he likes to pick his own. Maybe one of those GPS navigators for the Jag. He's always getting lost, and will never ask directions. Think they'd have that in small appliances up on six?"

"Sounds more like electronics to me."

"I don't see electronics," she observed.

"Let's try six," he said. "And if it's not there, an auto-supply store. Or Radio Shack."

"No way, hom-bré! You think Agèd Parent is going to have anything in his silver baby with red leather seats that says "Shack" on it? This is one of those Quest things... "

"Sharper Image catalogue?"

Since neither would admit to the other that they might prefer the elevator, they made their way up the stairs to the mezzanine, intending to hike the six flights. Back on the ground floor, there seemed to be some commotion, and they watched from a perfect observation post as things began to clarify.

Two men in weather-appropriate ski masks were quietly trying to make it clear to the poor jewelry maid, no doubt a seasonal hire from WSU, that it would be in everyone's interest (except Mister Kaufmann's) for her to hand over the contents of the locked gem cabinet. Another ski-masker watched the proximal crowd, while a fourth scanned for security, these latter two equipped with genuine automatic weapons. No alarm had sounded, at least publicly, and — short of some foolish heroic intervention on the part of the customers, Mister Kaufmann looked shortly to be out of several grand worth of rocks. The patrons close enough to see what was going on were frozen, not wanting to call the attention of the AK-47s. Those beyond visual contact were involved in the normal Brownian motion of crowded department stores. A small event was transpiring in the midst of a large non-event — that was all.

Richard and T.L., from their mezzanine perch noticed Santa quietly place the child on his lap down on the floor, whisper something in her ear, then stand and walk over to the four-seasons sportswear display. He took a hardball from April's mitt, a net from July's high-booted fisherman, drew a seven-iron from September's cart bag, and walked quietly to the edge of the stage, as if he were simply going to distribute these prizes to the line of waiting children. The property-is-theft ski-maskers seemed unaware. Santa was not one of their usual suspects.

Then, with a horrific AIIIEEEEE!, the red-suited fat man leaped far out from the edge of the stage, slamming down on number three's back, and whopping the landing net over his head, tugged hard enough to make him drop his gun. He kicked it away to a likely customer, who then covered the capturee. The second gunner turned toward his bearded target, and Santa fired a fastball right at his face. Again the gun was dropped and sequestered. The fat man charged the first of the jewel-seekers, and using a seven-iron to the head, disabled the other. The second gunman meanwhile, had charged him from behind, and distracted him enough for the first of the jewelers to turn back upon him. A two-on-one struggle ensued, with the appearance now of a Saturday night special, though it was only Thursday. Santa's stuffing was dragging from him like the eviscerations one might have seen in Quang Tri or Anbar Province. He pushed it in one attacker's face, spun and struck the pistoled hand of the other, and shoved the grip end of the iron into the testicles of the first. Karate chops to the necks of each finished all the action. On Mister Kaufmann's marble floor were three men in ski masks and an old Bauer .25. One other ski-masker was cowering before his own AK-47 in the hands of a macho-looking farmer who looked as if he knew how to use it. Its brother gun lay hidden under the parka of a blond Valkyrie who had snatched it up.

Done. Santa gathered up his belly, stuffed it back in, jumped back up on stage, sat down on his throne, and called out, "Next?" Security came, brought in the police and the EMTs, all was once again pax Christii, while the cash registers peeped everywhere, like a flock of angels.

"I couldn't have done it better myself," T.L. noted. "A regular Toshiro Mifune."

"The guy sure earns his pay," her cohort agreed.

They continued their climb to six, where they found that small appliances meant Cuisinarts and Mr. Coffees, and not cosmic connectors. But they both felt richer as they meditated on their day.

FIVE

A Radical is a Neocon Who's Been Mugged by Homeland Security

Speaking of Global Positioning, in mid-January, Richard and T.L. found themselves standing on the United line at the airport waiting to check-in for the 10:47 to Washington, DC. She was to give the keynote at the Heritage Foundation Annual Meeting, a $10K gig, the most she had ever made. There are advantages to preaching to the right choir. Going through Chicago, they were due in at 4:55, in good time for a high-class dinner and the speech. "Meetcha in Tehran, Hunan!" — her outrageous analysis of the US — China dynamic after Iranian liberation. That ought to earn her her supper, and set her up well for the next five-figured appearance. Nothing like épatez-ing the bourgeoisie.

And of course, standing on line at Wichita's Mid-Continent Airport, was a great opportunity for her *Ain't Nothin' The Matter With Kansas* research.

"Hey, I love your button!" she said to the forty-something little man in front of her. I ♥ MY MUSTANG, it said, with a graphic of low-slung snazz with broad yellow stripes down the hood. "I got one just like that."

"Really? A '69 Fastback?"

T.L. realized she might be in over her head.

"No, a button. The button you're wearing. I got one just like it."

"Oh. Great. But do you own a Stang?"

"I wish I could. Can't afford it."

Richard was enjoying the show. What a piece of chutzpah she was.

"And they're hard to come by in the blue states. I'm from Massachusetts. You can barely find one."

"Yeah, the blue states," he said. "What do they know about the fine points?"

"Like what?" she asked, flipping on the digital recorder in her parka pocket.

"Oh you know, out here we don't really know about wines or nannies or whaddya call it imperialism, but you know, our kids are great, I can wire my own house and fix my snowblower, my wife can cook circles around Julia Child, our church is always there for you, no matter what... "

She looked at Richard, to make sure he was hearing all this.

"We're not so smart, ironic, whatever, like they are, and... "

At which point the line moved forward, and he was called up to the counter.

"Hope you get your Stang someday. Nice talking to you."

She turned back to her companion.

"Is that a mensch — as your people would say? Is this guy — and his wife, and his kids and their church — mere grist for your buddy Tom Frank's mill?" She shut off the recorder.

And then it was their turn, the two of them, her Vuitton and his LL Bean.

"Has anyone but you packed your bags, Ma'am?"

"He helped me," she said, motioning back to Richard.

"And is he a relation?"

"Yes, I'm her husband," Richard the Gallant offered.

"He is not," she objected.

The ticket agent looked up from her computer.

"Well? Are you married, or are you not married?"

"Married/Not," they answered simultaneously.

By now, agents at neighboring counters were looking up.

"Look," Richard offered, "I mean we're on our way to our wedding at her parents' in DC."

The agent looked at the wedding-skimpy luggage.

"Wait just a minute," she said, and retired through the door behind the conveyor belt.

"Shall we split while we have a chance?" Richard asked.

"With those guys with the M-16s watching us because of your asshole joking around?"

"*My* joking around? You were the one who said I packed your bag."

"I said you helped, and you did. You leaned on it so I could close it. I'm a truth-teller — what are you? And besides, we have to get on the damn plane. Just let me handle it."

The agent returned with her supervisor, a large gray woman of the Mother Superior type.

"Please step over to the side, Ma'am, and you, too, Sir."

She gestured them out of the line and past the end of the ticket counter. The M-16 brigade followed them discreetly.

"Will we lose our place in line?" T.L. demanded. "We have to make this flight."

"If you're allowed to board, I assure you we'll get you on your flight."

"If? What do you mean, if? I'm the keynote speaker at a meeting toni... "

"Just calm down, Ma'am. May I see a photo ID? And yours, Sir? Thank you."

She held each of the cards to the scanning window of an elaborate PDA. The results she sought were available immediately.

"Look," T.L. said, "it was just a joke. I have this thing about, um, inefficient questions like 'did anyone besides you pack your bags.' If I'm a terrorist, what am I going to say, that yes, they were packed at... "

"We have to ask you these things. It's federal law."

"But it's idiotic, and... "

"Think what you like. Are you two married, or not?"

"Not," she said.

"Not," Richard added.

"Why did you say you were?"

"I didn't say it. He did."

"Why did *you* say you were?"

"He was just trying to..."

"I'm talking to him, not to you."

"I was just trying to make things go more quickly."

"By lying."

"I was just playing around."

"This is an airport. There is no playing around here. Do I have to explain?"

"OK, OK."

The Mother Superior place a red stick-on dot on their tickets, and dismissed the M-16s with a gesture of her head.

"We'll check you in as soon as your luggage has been thoroughly searched. Come with me, please."

She returned her customers to the ticket line, and handed the marked tickets to the agent, who rang for the baggage inspectors. At a side table, a man and a woman began to go through his and hers as if the luggage search were gender-sensitive.

"They're going to X-ray them later, right?" T.L. asked, "So why do you have to pull everything apart now?"

"Because you have red dots on your tickets," said the agent.

"I'd like to see the regs that require that." Any secret laws violate the Fifth Amendment's due process clause, as well as the constitutionally protected right to travel. She <u>had</u> gone to law school.

"You're not allowed to see them," the agent replied.

"Why can't you let me see them?"

"Because we don't have to. It's sensitive security information, and you're not allowed to see the regulations, nor is anybody else."

"Homeland pathology," Richard observed *sotto voce*. "It's simple Search and Destroy..."

"Not with me!" she hissed."

"Hey, that's what militias are trained to do. If they can sack Babylon, use the archeology for sandbags, they can certainly..."

"Babylon? Babylon? What the fuck is Babylon to you?"

All heads turned.

"What do you care about Babylon? You ever been there? If it disappeared today, every last ancient bit of it, would it make one iota of difference in your life? Liberal bullshit. Do you miss the dodo? The passenger pigeon? What the hell is the difference? Things vanish: so what?? Yes, history is bunk!"

The historian looked at his beloved. She was one pissed cookie.

Their luggage inspected and passed through the chute, their boarding passes in hand, they proceeded to security check-in, to be personally inspected, barefoot, beltless, and shorn of small appliances. In front of them in line was a young family loaded down with traveling accessories for three children — a stroller for the baby, a huge diaper bag, a cooler for fussy-kid food, a bag of books, games and toys, plus their own carry-ons waiting to be x-rayed. First through the metal detector was an ebullient four-year old who vaulted on through, pressing his hands against its sides as he swung his legs past the barrier. The barrier, naturally, protested, beeping away, violated and indignant. The small child was grabbed by Security1 and whisked off to the side to be thoroughly wanded, screaming with fright. His mom went off after him, only to be grabbed from behind by Security2, as the father, holding the baby, was fronted by Security3. "Don't touch him!" the mother was warned. "We'll handle this," the father was told. The detainee's big brother, only a year older, began wailing: "Abe! Little Abe! Oh, no, we loved him so much, and now we'll never see him again. "Quinn, Quinn, listen, it's all right," his father assured him. "Nothing is going to happen... " But the sight of Security3 guarding his father, and of Security2 holding back his screaming mother, and of Security1 poking his screaming little brother with an electric prod was not reassuring. The baby started to cry. Three loudly wailing children, a mother furiously protesting, a father arguing with security, the family spread out and isolated each from the other in the check-out area, their carry-ons strewn here and there — this was not the domestic tranquility sought by the founding fathers.

Into the fray jumped Teresa Lee Skulkington of the Connecticut Skulkingtons. She ran through the detector, setting it off with her speed, and grabbed at little Abe to try to return him to his TSA-restrained mother. But she herself was tackled by a young soldier in full riot gear who had leapt from his perch, loaded for bear, and rarin' to go: a pretty young woman was perfect. He seized her around the chest, pulled her buttocks tight against his groin, and held her there, quite pleased with himself, for capture. She reached her head around and bit his arm, as four white-shirted TSAers ran over to deploy. The burliest of them pulled her out of the soldier's arms, threw her in a painful hammerlock, and led her away. It took the other three to restrain Richard, but restrain him they did. The "good cop" of the crew advised him that just touching a federal officer is grounds for aggravated battery, a grave felony, not looked on lightly by the courts.

Teresa Lee Skulkington of the Connecticut Skulkingtons was strip-searched, and taken from the airport holding cell to the fifteenth precinct where she was booked, fingerprinted, and held in the drunk tank overnight for a felony bail hearing the next morning. She had missed her gig, ripped her blouse, soiled her name, and forfeited her honorarium. Lawrence Charles Skulkington of the Connecticut Skulkingtons had to wire $50,000 to spring his daughter after her assault on a federal officer. The trial was set for March.

The morning of her release, that very morning, she began to use the word "pigs" to refer to the police. Before this, like Blanche Dubois, she had always relied on the kindness of strangers.

SIX

Prairie Fire 1

12 January, 2006

My Dear Children,

It is heartening to hear of a second coming of freedom to Kansas. And gratifying too, it is to know your understanding of slavery admits not only slavery of the body, but slavery of the mind. Mine was the first victory; yours must be the second.
Well you fathom that it is a heinous, soul-damning sin to submit to laws and institutions condemned by conscience and reason. On this, do not be swayed. You must never obey a majority, no matter how large, if it oppose your principles and opinion, for the largest majority is often only an organized mob whose noise can no more change the false into the true than it can change black into white or night into day. And a minority — small, tiny, even the two of you — that minority conscious of its rights, if those rights are based on moral principles, will sooner or later become a just majority. What you are proposing here is nothing less than the free commonwealth promised us by our Declaration of Independence and prophesied and ordained by God in the Bible.
While you, Teresa, have your differences with Richard, as will always be the case, I must applaud your attack on the current worship of Santa Claus. A true commitment to God's map of this land, and not Satan's, must be the essential lode–stone for your journey. At the same time, I would advise you to dress more modestly, and not, as you did, to make such an address on the Sabbath. On the Sabbath, the Lord rested, and commanded you to do likewise, the better to reflect on Him. It is easy to be distracted in your modern, motorcycle-drawn life. The Sabbath will direct you to the rock and refuge of His throne.
And you, Richard, must beware the wiles of the university. The stinking dark–ness of institutionalized slavery had made Southerners into a foul and corrupt people. It had stolen their

souls and made them followers of Satan. A similar debasement threatens those who would profess their learning. Be not meek and self-protecting. Take care to teach not only your knowledge, but your passion; help fashion your pupils' stubbornness into principled belief, their willfulness into self-assurance.

For indeed the time is dire. The people refuse sound doctrine and turn away their ears from the truth. All is fable, and their mental slavery to these has made cowards of them all. And yet there is longing for spiritual immensity, for the unravelling of all the human tangles. And the Lord will protect His Children.

There is a man called by God, and his name is Richard. There is a woman called by God, and her name is Teresa. You are conscripts in the army of the Lord. If it be needed, go ye to commune alone with God. Keep ever fresh your sense of purpose. Find men of means ready to pay the expenses of your deeds, not as charity, but as wages.

There are only three paths: to submit, to fight, or to run away. I trust you will know the path which is yours. Slavery is the sum of all villainies, and its abolition the first essential work. Become the hands that once again free Kansas.

False are the men of high degree
The baser sort are vanity.
Laid in the balance both appear
Light as a puff of empty air.

I salute your wondrous love, unshrinking bravery, self-sacrificing benevolence, and devotion to the cause of freedom. May Heaven preserve your life and health, and prosper your noble purpose. If God be for us, who can be against us?

God is our all-sufficient aid.

Your friend,
John Brown

SEVEN

Santa Unbridled

"*Mrs. Skulkington?*"
"Ms. Skulkington."
"*Sorry. Ms. Skulkington, the GPS navigator you ordered is in.*"
"Thank you. I'll be by this week."
She clicked off the phone.
"Who was that?" Richard asked.
"Kaufmann's. They finally got Dad's Christmas present — only two weeks after Christmas."
"Well, now it can be a thank-you gift for his getting your case dismissed."
"It's called pull. It helps to have the Attorney General signing on. Still, he does like being extravagantly thanked."
"This should do it."
"What's up for you today?" she asked.
"Class at one, free after that."
"Shall we go by Special K and pick it up?"
"Sure. I'll be back a little after two."

January in Kansas can defeat the most intrepid biker. Today it was the wind. "Kansas" means "land of the wind." And even Wichita cannot ignore its place in a biblical land, a land of floods and droughts, locusts and prairie fire, twisters and "fraidy holes" to hide in, storm-breeding clouds twice the height of Everest, and prophets discharging underneath them. The guys at the Severe Storms Forecast Center are known as the "Keepers of the Gates of Hell." Richard and T.L. took the Chevy, and lucked into a meter right on the Kaufmann block.

The store was warm, the great ground-floor hall gaily enticing. Up on the stage, Santaland was still set up — in January! And on the throne, no red-robed elf, but a short black man in a blue serge suit sitting pre-schoolers on his lap.

Were there old Christmas carol tapes playing, now as depressing as they once were enchanting? No. Over the speakers, T.L. and Richard heard the great baritone preacher:

... This will be the day when all of God's children will be able to sing with a new meaning, "My country,

"Nice," said Richard.
"Bathetic cliché," said T.L.S.
He punched her shoulder, lovingly.

So let freedom ring in the two hundred choices of perfumes on our ground floor.

What?

Let freedom ring in the wide variety of bags and accessories. Let freedom ring in choosing from our latest shoe collections! Let freedom ring in Men's and Women's Sportswear! Let freedom ring in the curvaceous lines of our small appliances! And not only that; let freedom ring for the style-conscious mother-to-be! Let freedom ring for the little children, in Baby Basics and Cozies! Let freedom ring from every floor and counter at Kaufmann's. From every department, let freedom ring.

What the hell was going on?

And when we let freedom ring, we will be able to join hands and sing in the words of the old Negro spiritual, "Free at last! free at last! thank God Almighty, we are free at last!"

They looked at one another, each unable to speak. The loop cycled around, ignored by the multitude of shoppers — all but two.

... 'tis of thee, sweet land of liberty, of thee I sing. Land where my fathers died, land of the pilgrim's pride, from every mountainside, let freedom...

"Oh hi, Dr. Gronsky!"

A gorgeous young blond of the Kansas cheerleader type advanced on Richard, her coat over her arm, her cleavage declaiming from an unseasonable tanktop.

"Hi Jodi. Terry, this is Jodi McClain, one of my excellent students. Jodi, this is Terry Skulkington... "

The two women shook hands and eyed one another analytically.

"What's with this King parody?"

"Oh, don't you know? It's an old Kaufmann's tradition — a permanent Santa Claus for the kids. Except he's only Santa in December. Then he's Martin Luther King, and in February, Cupid, and in March, St. Patrick, I think, or maybe a leprechaun — like that."

"How old is old?" Richard asked.

"Last four or five years. You know — a fifth of my life."

"Shows you how often I come here."

"As Kansas goes, so goes the nation. When you see a full-time Santa at Bloomie's, you can say you were present at the creation."

"You really believe that?" T.L. asked. "As Kansas goes, so goes the nation?"

"Oh sure," Jodi assured her. "White Castle hamburgers started here, and Pizza Hut, and the first woman mayor, and the first democratic headquarters, and the first state mental institution. Hey, we started the Civil War."

"She's majoring in Kansas history," Richard noted, " — she ought to know."

"Interesting," T.L. said. "Bodes well for you, sweet." The "sweet" may have been for Jodi's ears. She had never called him "sweet" before.

"You mean for his Free State of Kansas?" Jodi asked.

"For <u>our</u> Free State of Kansas, yes. Are you involved?" T.L. asked.

"Laughable," Jodi said. "And he promised me he wouldn't lower my grade if I said that."

"You'll come round. I'm giving a talk about it at the Green Party meeting next week. Can you come?"

"When is it?"

"Tuesday, 7pm. Warwick 310. Can you come?"

"I'll check my calendar and let you know."

She touched his arm. There was an embarrassed silence.

latest shoe collections! Let freedom ring in Men's and Women's Sportswear! Let freedom ring in the curvaceous lines of our

"Well, I'll see you later. Nice to meet you."

"Likewise," said Teresa, noncommittally.

Jodi wandered off into the post-Christmas-sale crowd, putting on her coat, either because she was on her way out, or to combat T.L.'s iciness.

"Very interesting woman. Are all your students that pretty?"

"No. There are handsome Kansas studs too. Folks are good-looking out here, in a goyish sort of way."

"Goyish like me?"

"More innocent. You're not corn-fed. You've been to Yale. And don't be silly-jealous. Let's go check out Santa or whatever he is."

Scowling, she followed him through the crowd to the stage-end of the hall.

where my fathers died, land of the pilgrim's pride, from every mountainside, let freedom

They both studied the scene. On Santa's throne, now trimmed in black and white crepe paper, sat the short black, blue-serged man, slightly portly but still well-built, murmuring to a parka-bundled child on his lap. On either side of the proscenium arch hung fringed, winged monkeys, chimp-sized and slightly frightening. The store directory was still on display, but also trimmed in black and white. In fact, all red was gone from the scene. And green. The child left happily, jumped from the stage into a mommy's arms, and was replaced by another freckle-faced dumpling, slightly older.

"Is that the same guy?" T.L. whispered to her sweetie.

"I can't tell." Richard said. "Seems about the same size, but..."

"They wouldn't do blackface. In this day and age?"

"Maybe Santa was made up white... " he suggested.

The black man — who must be "Martin Luther King", who else? — mumbled something to the plumpling, the child stretched up to whisper something in his ear, and Dr. King broke out in a laugh so loud, it frightened her, and for a moment stopped all activity on the shopping floor. It was a strange kind of seal-like barking guffaw, effortless but convulsive, smacking of the maniac, accompanied by a flipperish whacking of his thigh with the hand not holding the child. The parents stepped closer to the stage. The child jumped down from his lap.

"Jeez!" Richard declared, "that must have been the tot-line of the century."

"Let's ask her what she said," T.L. added.

But they didn't. For the parents whisked her quickly away to un-laughing safety.

"Gone forever," T.L. said. "We'll never know."

ring in Men's and Women's Sportswear! Let freedom ring in the curvaceous lines of our small

"And what's with those monkeys? More subtle racist commentary to go along with the blackface?" She had come to the conclusion that it was makeup, well-applied.

"Actually, yes. Don't you recognize them?"

"I don't hang out with chimps," she said.

"The flying monkeys?"

ring for the little children, in baby basics and cozies ! Let freedom ring from every floor and counter at Kaufmann's

"Oh, my God, yes. It's the Wizard of Oz. The servants of the Wicked Witch of the West."

"I think they're a gift from MGM. At least that's what I've heard."

"How could I be so dumb?? Daddy read us the *Wizard* a million times, and we saw the movie over and over on its very first videotape. 'Toto, I don't think we're in Kansas anymore.'"

"Really? In your gated mansion? Wrong side of the class struggle, my dear."

"Liberal stereotyping. You don't know beans about the upper class."

"Well anyway, racist, yes," Richard continued, "though not against blacks. It was Baum's comment on the turn-of-the-century portrayal of Native Americans as monkeys. Enslaved monkeys."

"Get out!"

"No, really. Don't you know the real meaning of the story?"

"Don't give me any of your revisionist historian bullshit."

let freedom ring, we will be able to join hands and sing in the words of the old Negro spiritual, 'Free at last! free at last! thank God Almighty, we are

"Let's go up to the coffee-shop where we don't have to listen to this travesty, and I'll give you Frank Baum 101."

Now beyond showing off for one another, they took the elevator to the sixth floor.

able to join hands and sing in the words of the old Negro spiritual, 'Free at last! free at last! thank God Almighty, we are

"Well, guess not," Richard observed, pointing at the loudspeakers. T.L. rolled her eyes.

Coffee and crullers in hand, they settled into the only empty booth.

liberty, of thee I sing. Land where my fathers died, land of the pilgrim's pride, from every mountainside

"I bet when you came you knew only two things about Kansas — *In Cold Blood*, and *The Wizard of Oz*."

"Three. '*I'm as corny as Kansas in August...* '" she sang.

The other customers turned round.

"Ok, ok," he shusshed, a little embarrassed. And I'm sure you've got Truman Capote down. But in spite of Daddy's leftwing bed-time stories, you still don't get *The Wizard of Oz*. Look — you ready for this?... "

"I'll take a coffee and cruller's worth, and let you know."

"Baum published it in 1900, in the midst of a Populist campaign against corruption. The Populist Party. People were demoralized or muzzled, just like now, public opinion was silent, midwestern land was had been bought up by capitalists, there were big anti-union drives, pauperized labor was being used to beat the farmers and workers down, and colossal fortunes were being built up on the backs of the poor. Paupers and millionaires — the American people. Baum was pissed. You with me?"

"For the moment."

"So he wrote this wonderful allegory of social, economic and political affairs at the turn-of-the-century.'

"Who beside you thinks this?"

"Scholars, my dear, many historians and scholars. Besides, look at the story: a road of gold bricks leading to a green city by a fraud whose power is in secrecy and spin? Wicked witches on the east and west coasts; good witches in the Populist, agrarian heartland, north and south? A worker turned by industrial wickedness from a human being into a heartless, rusting machine? Farmers without brains enough to scare away the crows that pick them bare? Powerful people who should be in charge too cowardly to assert their power? The little people, Munchkins, enslaved by the east? The yellow Winkies enslaved by the west? The monkeys? The poppies? Oz is a confusing, alienating, and dangerous, if beautiful, world, not unlike our own."

"But Dr. Gronsky, my dear, why should your proletarian heroes head toward a phony to make them whole? Why choose to travel a road of pestilent yellow bricks to the tawdry green-jeweled city? *'We're off to see the wizard, the wonderful...'*" She sang again. "Why?"

"Why, indeed? The question answers itself. Look around you."

freedom ring, we will be able to join hands and sing in the words of the old Negro spiritual

"Baum was an artist, not a propagandist." Richard continued. "Why were there happy endings in Dickens? Yes, the Wizard turns out to be benevolent — recognizing Scarecrow's real intelligence, Tin Man's real capacity for feeling, and Lion's real courage. In the Populist tradition, he empowers ordinary people with their own enduring common sense, compassion and guts. The political allegory is in a dance with a good story. Maybe it's just a little 'nicey-nice', maybe it represents a deeper understanding, more

optimistic, of the struggle between humanity and power. But the master story, of course is that of finding home.
> *We shall not cease from exploration*
> *And the end of all our exploring*
> *Will be to arrive where we started*
> *And know the place for the first time."*

"Little Gidding," she noted.

"You get an A for recognition — but there Dorothy is, where she started, back in a country divided into sections and warring races, and the questions remain: Why are good people ruled by bad rulers, why, even, is Kansas, the heartland, such an unhappy place? Dorothy's real problems don't begin with the tornado, but when she gets back home."

the curvaceous lines of our small appliances! And not only that

"I'll think about it," T.L. said.

"You want to finish your coffee and cruller?"

"No."

They bussed their dishes, and went to claim their Global Positioning System.

EIGHT

What Do Kansans Love?

February — from *februa*, "means of cleansing", a purificatory and expiatory time, even in Kansas. One Isadore of Seville conceived the god Februus, whom he associated with Pluto, god of the underworld, and Kansans thank the Lord that hellish February is short, if not sweet.

And yet they know that February's last big snow, lying still deep on the land, will fill the aquifers and reservoirs, freshen the streams, and moisten the soil for their crops. So hated, yet needed, February runs along through past presidents, and Lent, and the north winds raging.

Enter St. Valentine, martyr. 269 AD was a bad year for folks of that name, as two Valentines seem to have been martyred, though legend has conflated them into one. The story goes that Emperor Claudius II had decreed that Roman soldiers were not to marry or become engaged. Divided loyalties and family expenses — bad. The insouciant Father Valentine took to secretly marrying them anyway — sacrament over soldierdom. He was discovered, arrested, imprisoned and liquidated on February 14th. A not very romantic end.

In the great melange of human imagination and confusion, standing in the wings, as it were, was Cupid-Eros, son of Mars and Venus, Ares and Aphrodite, still wet with Lupercalia:

Saynt Valentyne, of custume yeere by yeere,
Men haue an vsavnce in this Regyoun
To looke and serche Cupydes Kalundere,
And cheese theyre choys by gret affeccioun;
Suche as beon pricked by Cupydes mocion,
Taking theyre choyse, as theyre soort dothe falle
But I loue oon whiche excellithe alle.

(John Lydgate, 1395)

His sprouting wings may have arrived via the ornithology of the Renaissance poets. Chaucer writes of ... *Seynt Valentyne's day*
...Whan every foul cometh ther to choose his mate, and Herrick ups the ante in a Valentine day come-on to his lover:
Oft have I heard both Youths and Virgins say,
Birds chuse their Mates, and couple too, this day...
Virgin, beware.

Kaufmann's Department Store was not enamored of St. Valentine, martyr, but preferred the warmer, fuzzier incarnation as Cupid. And a Cupid, or at least some cupid-like being occupied Santa's heart-embellished throne when T.L. and Richard arrived for the first of their projected monthly checks.

The loudspeakers' loop eternal:
How do I love thee? Let me count the ways.
I love thee from the depth and breadth and height of Kaufmann's.
I might love thee with a Chambray Handkerchief quilt from our domestics department, fifth floor.
My very soul might reach for thine in a rugged Italian fatigue sweater in brown or black. Mensware, third floor.
I'd love thee in an Icelandic Leaf Zip pullover, in colors to match your hair. Womensware, second floor.
I love thee freely, as men strive for right — using chrome precision desk accessories by El Casco, fourth floor. My love is as pure Crabtree & Evelyn,
I love thee with the breath of Shalimar... Smiles, tears, of all my life, all here, for you, at Kaufmanns.

Again, they couldn't believe it. Who was writing these things? T.L. ripped out her back-pocket pad and copied it down for her book notes. Kansans do love hearts and cupids.

They made their way over, close to the stage, and inspected Cupid carefully. A little oversized for a babe, but as a winged, adolescent Eros, passable. He was dressed in Batman-ish, skin-colored tights with barely-visible hems fading well into his own bare hands and feet. He looked athletic, but was expertly padded — just enough to suggest an archetypal Cupidian chubbiness. An adult diaper completed the effect. And the wings, invisibly mounted.

Was it the same person? His height was similar, but his total appearance so different — portliness, costume, pigmentation — that they were hard put to say — until he gave a childish, chastised version of that original mammoth-seal laugh, complete with flapping right flipper. Then they knew they had their man. They were on to him.

As were probably many other customers. For Kansans love a good gag. Here's one:

Old Indian story: The white man asked, *Where is your nation?* The red man said, *My nation is the grass and rocks and the four-leggeds and the six-leggeds and the belly wrigglers and swimmers and the winds and all things that grow and don't grow.*

Well, maybe that's not so funny. In any case, Kansans do love a good gag. Take the state flower, *Helianthus annuus*, the giant sunflower. Is it to celebrate the Kansas sunshine? Hardly. In the summer, prairie temperatures can get to the hundred and teens in the shade, and west of Wichita shade is hard to come by. No, as an 1887 editorial in a Kansas paper put it,

> *They call Kansas "the Sunflower State, not because it is overrun with the noxious weed, but because, as the sunflower turns on its stem to catch the first beams of the morning sun, and with its broad disk and yellow rays follows the great orb of the day, so Kansas turns to catch the first rays of every advancing thought or civilized agency, and with her broad prairies and golden fields welcomes and follows the light.*

Perhaps it takes a Kansan to appreciate the irony: you have to have been there. Witness the state motto: *"Ad astra per aspera"* — to the stars through adversity. That's a pretty good one. The historian Alan Nevins once observed,

> *"Kansas has been the testing ground for every experiment in morals, politics, and social life. Doubt of all existing institutions has been respectable. Nothing has been venerated or revered merely because it exists or has endured. Prohibition, female suffrage, fiat money, free silver, every incoherent and fantastic dream of social improvement and reform, every economic delusion that has bewildered the foggy brain of fanatics, every political fallacy nurtured by misfortune, poverty, and failure, rejected elsewhere, has here found tolerance*

and advocacy. The enthusiasm of youth, the conservatism of age, have alike yielded to the contagion, making the history of the State a melodramatic series of cataclysms, in which tragedy and comedy have contended for the mastery, and the convulsions of Nature have been emulated by the catastrophes of society. There has been neither peace, tranquility or repose."

As I say, Kansans love a good gag.

My very soul might reach for yours in a rugged Italian fatigue sweater...

Oh, shut up.

Kansans also love the sky. They have to. A Kansan tourist to Vermont was asked, "What do you think of the scenery?" "There isn't any," she replied. "The mountains get in the way."

Kansans are a race of sky-watchers. Most mornings, a huge geography begins in the faintest shades of pink, then moves to oranges and crimsons, then into the pale yellow of the morning sun. And nowhere in the world, they say, is the morning sky such an innocent blue, and nowhere is the sunset more awesome: a burning globe paints the land with phosphorescence as it sinks below the far horizon. And that sky teaches, too, a chronic awareness of the unexpected, and an awed respect for natural forces which can overwhelm and destroy. The thrill of lack of restraint, a haunt of uproar. That too, Kansans love.

So, uproarious, perhaps, in a tiny way, was February's cupidic Santa. At least Richard and Teresa thought he was, and they weren't even Kansans. *Cupidus* means "desiring".

It may sound preposterous, but after their first monthly Santa check, they went right home and made love. Afterwards, in the late afternoon sunset, they walked the streets of Old Town. The People of the Wind were bundled up against it.

Most Kansans do not love February.

NINE

The Wheel

*If the doors of perception were cleansed
everything would appear to man as it is, infinite.*
                    William Blake

It was March. They knew it was March because forsythias were thinking yellow. They knew it was March because it was pinkish light when they awoke and the thermometer fluctuated wildly day to day. They knew it was March because the queer old balloon man was whistling far and wee in the background, and because the flickers knew it, too. But most of all they knew it was March because Kaufmann's stage was decked in green and shamrocks, and the loudspeakers were cycling the following:

*Turning and turning in the widening gyre
Come see the falcon in our aviary, sixth floor.
Things fall apart; but Craftsman tools repair them,
And all our items come with warrantees.
The ceremony of innocence occurs in bridal-wear, fourth floor,
for lovers full of passionate intensity.
Surely a Second Coming is at hand. And a third. And a fourth.
Earn Kaufmann points with each and every purchase.
And in the petting zoo, sixth floor, our rough beast, Dolly-lama,
wants your love. Parental supervision required.*

And Santa was looking like some odd cross between the venerable St. Patrick and some kind of herpetological leprechaun, embroided with iconic snakes.

It was more than March: it was the vernal equinox, Bach's birthday, a day which Richard celebrated annually by listening to all of the Matthew Passion. This year, however, most passion was turned toward a certain Teresa Lee Skulkington of the Connecticut Skulkingtons, his main squeeze and his addiction, his teammate and his opponent, the woman who came to dinner. Nevertheless, Bach was Bach, and not to be neglected.

After a spring fertility meal (condoms plus cream tonight) at Single Pebble, <u>the</u> great Old Town Chinese restaurant — spring rolls, steamed asparagus salad with ginger-lemon dressing, Royal Bird's Nest for her, Ants Crawling Up A Tree for him, kumquats for both for dessert — they walked home for the promised evening of their Savior's pain, death and resurrection. They settled in, took off their shoes, and Richard fetched his beloved Scherchen recording (Hughes Cuenod, Evangelist extraordinaire!), and placed the first disc in the machine. Teresa fiddled meanwhile in one of her drawers.

"Here!" she exclaimed. "Let's do this, instead."

"What?"

Richard looked up from the play button.

"This. My personal Grateful Dead medley. I burned it for you before I left."

"You mean instead of Bach? Or as some kind of prelude?"

"Instead."

"But it's his birthday... "

"Yes, and I brought you — now that I think of it — a Bach's birthday present."

"Well, thank you, but... "

"And it requires the Dead."

"Well, ok, but then we'll do the Passion? It's almost three hours long... "

"Sure, sure. Afterwards."

She went to the machine, installed her own CD instead of his, and turned back to her perplexed friend.

"Now close your eyes and stick out your hand."

"Come on!"

"No, really."

He did as he was told by the woman who must be obeyed. She reached into her pocket.

"There. You can look."

In his hand lay a small glassine envelope marked "U.S.P.S." Inside lay what looked like a small copy of some Andy Warhol Uncle Sam, multiple tiny images offset shoulder to head, shoulder to head, each Sam divided into hat, face and body by microperforations.

"I didn't know Warhol did Uncle... "

"It's not Andy Warhol."

"Who, then?"

"It's not art, it's truth — if you'll permit the distinction."

Richard drew the two inch square out of its envelope, and regarded it carefully. It seemed to be printed on some kind of blotter paper from the pen and ink days.

"Wait a minute!" he said, "Is this... ?"

"What do you think? And still undetectable by pigland airport security."

"For me? For Bach's birthday?"

"For us. Four hits for you, five for me."

"But I'm twice as heavy as you."

"Wrong. I'm twice as heavy as <u>you</u>. And I bet I've done more acid. And I bet I can handle it better."

"Well, it's true I've... "

"It's all right."

"But I once tried some... "

"You're a good boy. We deadheads prefer lysergic acid diethylamide."

"<u>You're</u> a deadhead?"

She stuck her thumbs into proud-position in her imaginary vest.

"Teresa Lee neé Skulkington, daughter of Lawrence Charles Skulkington, of the Connecticut Skulkingtons?"

She nodded.

"At parties inside your gated Westport community?"

"When Mommy and Daddy were in Europe — which was often."

"Oh."

He looked at his improbable partner.

How can I keep your soul from touching mine?

"Don't worry. I can guide you through. Trust me. Now stick out your tongue. Maybe we should start with three."

She carefully tore along the perforations.

"One... complete... Uncle... Sam. There! He'll prefer that to being dismembered."

"What about you?"

She downed her scheduled five, leaving a solo Samface which she push-pinned to the bulletin board in the kitchen, and returned with two glasses of Chardonnay. He accepted his wine with love and admiration in his eyes.

"OK. You look transformed already," she said. "Have you partaken yet?"

He shook his head, and displayed his strip of Uncle Sam.

"Well, just stick it under your tongue for a minute or so, then you can wash it down with your vino."

She reached for the play button.

"Wait," he interrupted. "Can we just hear the first chorus of the Bach — just in case we don't get to it? Tomorrow isn't his birthday anymore. It's only ten minutes. Eleven."

"Go for it."

He took the abandoned cd from the top of the box where she had placed it, traded it with hers in the machine, hit play, and settled in for a micro-hit of spiritual coitus-to-be-interruptus.

The dark and pulsing E minor, velvety yet terrifying, so truthful to the painful story of the world. *Come, daughters of men, help me to lament!* Evocative, intertwined wailing of the still-living human damned. *Look! The Bridegroom comes. How does He come? Like a lamb to slaughter.*

And then the incredible, cruel contrast — the voices of children declaiming the innocence of the Lord, the first phrase of "Oh, Lamb of God, Most Holy", an island of light floating in the Styx of human darkness.

Richard reached over and hit STOP.

"What's the matter? You're right. It's terrific."

"Yeah, I... "

"What?"

"It's too much now. Maybe it's doing this with you when I've been doing it alone for so many years. I don't know. Maybe it's Uncle Sam kicking in... We can do it for Bach's half-birthday in September. I always thought autumnal darkening was more appropriate anyway."

"Have it your way."

He placed the Bach disc in its box, and substituted Teresa's in the machine.

"Now?"

"Sure. Put it on repeat, or whatever, so it will cycle around."

They settled in, snuggling, to wait for the train to arrive. She sang along, while he listened.

What do you want me to do to see you throoooooo?

"Just be here with me."

And she was.

Waiting, waiting, waiting for Godot.

"Anything happening yet?" she asked.

"Not yet." he said. "You?"

She patted him on the knee, and left for the kitchen to prepare some snacks.

A friend of the devil is a friend of mine.

"Is that you?" he yelled from the living room.

"What?" she yelled back.

"A friend of the devil."

"What do you think?"

She reappeared with a plate of chips and guacamole.

"Do thou, then, renounce the devil and all his works, and the vain pomp and glory of the world, with all covetous desires of the same, and the sinful desires of the flesh, so that thou wilt not follow nor be led by them!"

"Where the hell'd you get that?"

"Made it up."

"You did not."

"Did."

"Well, I'm not going to. Renounce anything." She pecked him at the groin. "Here. Check out the news, while I slip into something more comfortable."

Got some things to talk about, here, beside the rising tide...

Richard perused the *Eagle*, and found himself skipping the latest news from Iraq. Maybe he'd already read it.

"Listen to this," he called into the bedroom. Some high school student in Lawrence did a Science Fair project to show how easy it was to manipulate Americans about science. He distributed a flyer about dihydrogen monoxide... "

"What's that?"

"Water, you dope."

"I knew it was water.'"

"... which claimed that quote 'prolonged exposure to its solid form caused severe tissue damage, that exposure to its gaseous form caused severe burns and that it had been found in tumors from terminal cancer patients. 86% of the 50 students he surveyed thought dihydrogen monoxide should be banned.'"

"Yeah. Well, I'd worry more about the millions of Americans... " — she came back into the living room. Her "something more comfortable" was her black leotards and tanktop — "who claim to have been abducted by aliens."

"They have, of course — the Neocons."

"Fuck you, typical liberal pig. Hey, anything happening yet?"

Richard did seem somewhere else.

"What?"

"You still with us? How ya doing? Anything happening yet?"

I can't help you with your trouble if you won't help me with mine.

"I can't help you with your trouble if you won't help me with mine," he said.

"I don't have any trouble — except you."

"How come you brought me acid? I mean you — Ms. Upper Class Important Family Proper?"

"What's so surprising? Herman Kahn was an acid head. He used to lie around on the floor, murmuring 'Wow!'"

"How do you know?"

"Friend of Daddy's. Told us about it at dinner."

"No, really. What's with the psychedelics? How'd you get into them?"

"What is this, some kind of gender-oppression? Psychedelic means mind-manifesting. Women are not supposed to have minds? Is this a typical liberal position? Well, just think of them as this housewife's better broom to sweep the circuits clean."

"I don't think of you as the housewifely type."

"Yeah, you and all the others."

"What do you mean?"

On the day that I was born, daddy sat down and cried

"I mean all the guys who test drove and never purchased. I mean like I somehow I became some sort of Skulkington Finishing School for rich fraternity jocks. They were all so thankful. I have a collection of touching communications, hand-written and emailed. 'Terry, I'm really so grateful for our time together. It's so great with Mindy now thanks to all you taught me...'"

"Better that than hate."

"Why the fuck should they hate me?"

"Well, I mean..."

"Yeah, yeah.

It happens in meiosis, Milly,
All those genes ain't there..."

"C'mon, be reasonable."

"Nothing is reasonable. Nothing!"

She turned away from him.

"Sorry," she said.

"That's ok. It's fine." He stroked her angel-blond hair where it fell spectacularly across her black tanktop.

They sat in silence for a while.

The first days are the hardest days.

While tripping can be most intense and interesting for the traveller, it is usually far less so for the looker-on. Because we're in the home of a history professor, and because T.L. is leafing through his copy of *A Picture History of Bleeding Kansas*, it behooves us to fill the reader in on key events in the story of Kansas, a history not irrelevant to the fate of our heroes. For wheels turn here, too.

The Plot

Westward Ho! Look at this, all up for grabs:

The size of the United States doubled at the stroke of Jefferson's pen. 530 million acres at 3¢ an acre. Is that a deal? What would become the states of Louisiana, Missouri, Arkansas, Iowa, North Dakota, South Dakota, Nebraska, and Oklahoma, plus most of Kansas, Colorado, Wyoming, Montana, and Minnesota was up for grabs in "the territories". Let's go!

But who is <u>we</u>? There were already two quite different regions of the "United" States — the agricultural, slave-holding south, and the free, more industrial north. Attitudes and fortunes were tied up in this division. So who is "we", and what kind of economy would "we" establish? What manner of "civilization"? The stage was set over half a century for "Bleeding Kansas", and the Civil War.

"Anything yet?" he asked her.

"Maybe. You? What are you feeling right now?"

"A little tingly. Head and hands. And if I'm quiet, the room feels like it's breathing."

"With your breath?" she asked.

"Maybe. Let's see."

Richard did three deep in- and exhalations, and burst out laughing. "My god, I'm the room! Ve-ry weird."

He began to examine his new, larger room-self, its colors, its angles, its surfaces and cracks — cracks which were also connections — within and across all planes, walls behind walls, the sky behind the sky, a sudden penetration of all things around, strange more than beautiful. And with this exploration, there came a sense of exaltation, of immense joyousness, so...

Cosmic Charlie, how do you do?
Go on home, your mama's callin' you.
"I'm Cosmic Charley! I am!"

Cosmic Charley broke out in huge laughter, barking, sealish, unlike any sound Richard Gronsky had ever made. Cosmic Charley spread out over the world, inviolate, laughing and laughing at the trivial enthrallments so urgently worried by the *Wichita Eagle*. He sang in his leonine cosmic voice
If I were King of the Forest,
Not queen, not duke, not prince...
and cracked up again, roaring and guffawing
I'd click my heels and the trees would kneel...
Teresa put her hand on his shoulder.
"Steady, boy."

"I'm going to be King of Kansas. I'm going to free Kansas," he assured her. His pupils, if not his artillery, were now twelve gauge. He took her hand and looked hard at Terry. "I am."

But Terry was not quite Terry, for her face began to melt and change into a succession of phantasmagorical personae. It, itself, began to breathe and undulate, to liquefy before his very eyes. A stream of faces flowed in and out of her, the faces of all women, young and old, beautiful and hideous, comforting and bizarre, known and imponderable, the whole evolutionary history of female. She quickly grew a snout, and then she didn't. A field of energy surrounded her head, darting out splinters of multicolored light like fireworks, filling the room with sparkles, illuminating infinity, hilariously lovely and frightening.

"I'm here," she assured him.

The Cast of Characters

Slave or free? There is another category, archetypally American: "All I want to know is what's in it for me and mine?" And man by man, family by family, this may have been the most common impetus — the kind that would disappoint and frustrate John Brown. Nevertheless, floating like immiscible croutons in this predictable human soup were at least three other sharply-defined groups of ideologues.

1. The Slavers and "Border Ruffians", the former relative aristocracy (like Simon Legree), the latter, their redneck minions, largely fueled by alcohol.

A picture is worth a thousand words:

2. The Abolitionists. The most famous, of course, were the New Englanders, who migrated for the specific purpose of populating the territories with free-staters, many aided financially and logistically by the New England Emigrant Aid Society. The non-pacifists among them had supplements from the Rev. Henry Ward Beecher's congregation in Brooklyn — crates full of the new-style, breech-loading Sharps rifles that could fire ten accurate rounds a minute — shipped in cases marked "Bibles". The owners of "Beecher's Bibles" were John Brown's most likely adherents.

But there were other abolitionists with different motives, different goals. Far less puritanical, somewhat more selfish, but no less radical were the southern proles who, after being oppressed by the aristocracy with its black, free labor, wanted nothing more than a cast-free society and an economic system that would not exclude them. They blamed slavery for the hard life they had been forced to bear, and wanted that peculiar institution abolished. But many, raised in the south, were racists or separatists. They wanted no slavery — <u>and</u> they wanted no blacks. Let them go live elsewhere.

An odd hybrid of forces. The total situation was explosive.

"I'm here," she assured him.

But was she really? For she too, had entered a different part of the labyrinth.

The wheel is turning and you can't slow down,
You can't go back and you can't hold on,
You can't go back and you can't stand still,
If the thunder don't get you then the lightning will.

Her body was vibrating with an intense energy — five Uncle Sams worth. She could literally feel the music on her skin, and then could taste it and smell it.

Won't you try just a little bit harder,
Couldn't you try just a little bit more?

Richard was floating back through childhood and beyond.

"I fall down steps and kill Iself," he said.

Won't you try just a little bit harder,
Couldn't you try just a little bit more?

"I love them all, all of them, every..."

He began to weep uncontrollably.

"Now don't break down on me and go all gooey about the Brotherhood of Man!" she warned.

And for her, with every downbeat, a splash of fractal webbing would illuminate the room, a moire of multicolored connections. Every echoed obbligato of the lead guitar shifted the focus and intensity, tracing its line in n-dimensional space. The spirits of ancient dead from Egypt, China, India, sang in three-part harmony

Won't you try just a little bit harder,
Couldn't you try just a little bit more?

"Yes," she thought, "I can, I can."

Life in all its aspects <u>was</u> worth living, divinely beautiful and significant. Though she had glimpsed it before, if rarely, she now experienced a vision from the inner world — that Love, the One Thing, the Holy Thing, was the primary and fundamental cosmic fact. She felt herself growing ever-softer, wiser and less cock-sure, free from the mold life had set around her. The world could be changed, <u>would</u> be changed. Patriotism wasn't enough. Neither was anything else. Politics, economics, science, art, duty, action, contemplation — nothing short of <u>everything</u> would really do. For the first time ever while tripping, she cried — for joy. Through her tears, a miraculous, looking-glass world.

"My right side is my left side, and my left side is my right!" Most confusing. The glory in the clear light of the Void.

You can't let go and you can't hold on,
 You can't go back and you can't stand still,

Teresa Lee Skulkington of the Connecticut Skulkingtons.

If the thunder don't get you then the lightning will.

Four Dates and Three Acts
1. <u>1820 The Missouri Compromise</u> allowed Maine to enter the union as a free state, and Missouri as a slave state — but that henceforth slavery would be barred from the rest of the Louisiana Purchase north of Missouri's northern border. The Compromise Act would appear to have settled the slavery-extension issue.

2. <u>1850 The Fugitive Slave Act.</u> Two systems, and a one-way underground railroad from one to the other. The American worship of "property". Ay, there was the rub. Northerners legally required to aid in the capture and return of escaped slaves. The Abolitionist movement heated up, the railroad passengers increased, countermanding northern-state laws were passed, sectional hostility became more bitter, and the controversy over slavery in the territories was reunited.

3. <u>1854 The Kansas-Nebraska Act.</u> Democracy, Democracy! In a cleverly spun repeal of the Missouri Compromise, The Democratic Congress voted in <u>territorial</u> decision concerning the status of slavery. "Let the People decide!" The sponsors claimed their "doctrine of popular sovereignty" would arrest the "torrent of fanaticism" dividing the nation. Instead, northern free-soilers formed armed emigrant associations, and pro-slavers

sent settlers — bogus and real — pouring over the border from Missouri to vote. With the passage of the Kansas-Nebraska Act, the stage was set for murderous mob rule in the territory of Kansas. All chance of compromise was gone.

4. <u>1857 The Dred Scott Decision.</u> Scott, a Missouri slave who had briefly lived in the free state of Illinois, and the Wisconsin Territory (free under the provisions of the Missouri Compromise), was brought back to Missouri by his master, and then sued for his freedom on the grounds that his northern residencies had made him a free man, and with northern lawyers, took the case all the way to the Supreme Court. The court denied him his freedom. Chief Justice Roger B. Taney wrote that Negroes "had no rights which any white man was bound to respect." And furthermore, the Court went on to declare that the Missouri Compromise was unconstitutional because slaves were property, and masters were guaranteed their property rights under the Fifth Amendment. Neither Congress nor a territorial legislature could deprive a citizen of his property without due process of law. The South hoped that the decision would mark the end of antislavery agitation. The effect was rather the opposite.

And at the seventh hour, they rested. The Dead cd had been retired. Richard lay sprawled out on the couch, eating green, green guacamole, singing to himself his favorite verse from Carmina Burana over and over like some tape loop at Kaufmann's.

Rex sedet in vertice
Caveat ruinam!
Mmmm, mmmm, mmm, yowsa...
Nam sub axe legimus
Hecubam reginam.
"Yes."

She, on the other hand, was over-tired-revved, sitting in the chair, her arms around her knees, her head down, wrapped in teeming brain.

"You know that article you read me?"

"Unh unh."

"The article about the kid and the water?"

"No. What kid? What water?"

"Hydrogen oxide or whatever."

"Oh, yeah, yeah. What about it?"

"The Free State of Kansas is never going to happen... "

"What do you mean?" he loudly objected.

"Hold on there. Hear me out, hear me out."

Richard closed his eyes.

"The Free State of Kansas is never going to happen — without some kind of shock, some huge consciousness-raising about the true state of things."

"Isn't Dubya enough?"

"No, no, no. Read your own goddamn Frank book. Rove has got the status quo sewn up. We've got to break... "

"Could we talk about this tomorrow?"

"This *is* tomorrow. Look at the sky. And you've got an eight o'clock class. So perk up!"

She poured what was left of the chardonnay in his lap.

"Look," she continued, "the American public is very sweet — especially Kansans — and Love is All — and all — but they're... I don't want to say 'stupid'. Let's just say they're a little hidebound in what they take to be the present. The official version of the present."

"Let's give 'em all some Uncle Sam... " he suggested.

"Yeah, well they've had too much Uncle Sam already. They need to — what do you academics say? — unpack him. See what's really in there."

"But that's ridiculous. They won't," Richard observed.

"They will if they are shaken up enough. Enough to see through some of the more obvious lies."

"Like?"

"Like all the 9/11 stuff, liberal bonehead. What could be more explosive?"

"They've already *been* shaken up by 9/11."

"Yeah, and they've circled the wagons. Around Dubya and the gang."

"That's predictable. People always support..."

"But what if they realized that Dubya and the gang were the ones that did it? I mean in some way did it?"

"What?"

"9/11."

"Unh unh. I'm not going there. And no one else will either."

He rose exhaustedly to his feet and began pacing.

"Look," she lectured, "who ordered NORAD to stand down? Have you seen the early photos of the Pentagon? It's only a little, tiny hole. Where's the plane? Melted? Where are the engines? Engines don't vaporize from burning fuel. How did two giant skyscrapers..."

"Three."

"Three — collapse from fire when no steel buildings had ever collapsed lake that before in the history of buildings? C'mon. Weren't you suspicious when you saw all that on TV?"

"No. I was horrified."

"Hey, these are the guys that took us into war to stop Saddam from dropping nuclear bombs on us. And they've got people still swallowing it."

"<u>These</u> are the guys?? These are your buddies, your father's friends. I can't believe you're saying this! You! Ms. Fierce Right-wingnut."

"Yeah. Well that was then and this is now. Post. Don't you want to see the Free State of Kansas?"

"Yes, of course."

"So we need to shake our dear citizens out of their lethargy. Fight the mass psychosis."

"How?"

Teresa sat down in Richard's place.

"I don't know."

"Good."

"But I do know this: Things seem pretty benign here at home, right? — at least for Dubya and the gang. But a haystack soaked with kerosene also looks benign. It doesn't smell that way — but then neither does the country. But it <u>appears</u> content to just sit there — until you toss in a match."

"And you want to be the match."
"<u>We</u> want to be the match."
"The 9/11 stuff."
"What else? It's the smoking gun."
"I see."

Richard plopped down next to her on the couch. They both sat in silence for several minutes, each concerned with conflagration.

"What was that place called with the French name that John Brown... where somebody slaughtered somebody else?" she asked out of the blue.

"Marais des Cygnes," he answered, Swamp of the Swans. Why? You thinking of slaughtering somebody? Your once-beloved vice-president, when he comes to speak at Raytheon next week?"

"No," she said, taking him seriously. "That would bring down a police state big time. Homeland Security über Alles. No, we need some kind of teaching moment. And it can't be seen as a terrorist act."

"A teaching moment."

"You're supposed to know about those. I just thought it was a nice name."

"What?"

"Marais des Cygnes."

"Oh."

"It's like you and me. You the swamp, and I the swan.

TEN

She Leaves a Note

A LATE VALENTINE'S ODE TO THE AMPERSAND & YOU

If you the swamp & I the swan
Let's see how others are getting on:

There's nothing made by cyclotron
Like Vladimir & Estragon.

The Ranger yelled out "Heigh-ho Silver"
But couldn't fly like Orville & Wilbur.

Gods with not one foot of clay
Were our great leaders, Bob & Ray.

Though often seeming kinda wiggy
Role models they, Kermit & Piggy.

Though resolutely nothing phony
They're strangely named, Lingam & Yoni.

Nuttier than wing or filbert
Were Sullivan & his buddy, Gilbert.

Partners they on one strange journey,
But always fighting, Bert & Ernie.

Their little jokes were not so fonny
Still, who could rival Clyde & Bonnie?

But then there are, by gum, by golly
Those comic masters, Stan and Ollie.

And at the fair, ensconced with piemen,
Garfunkle & comrade, Simon.

And in their mansion, most hob-nobbin'
The doughty sleuths, Batman & Robin

Their thinking, p'raps, a little hazy,
We celebrate Ignatz & Krazy.

Kierkegaard may suffer dread
But not when watching Ginge & Fred.

Do they rhyme with 'clean' or 'fine' —
Richard Rodgers & Hammerstein?

Patriots will never love it,
That unAmerkin Bread & Puppet.

Please let no more stand in the way
Of sweet Bouvard & Pécuchet.

One charming dope, and one fine fellow,
The yin/yang Abbot & Costello.

Henri Beyle, he was no hack,
Especially The Red & Black.

She Leaves A Note

At home in neither house nor rancho,
The complementary Don & Sancho.

Something homey, something lacy,
The most un-PC George & Gracie.

Snoopers among jetsam, flotsom,
The legendary Holmes & Watson.

But lest competition may cause you to sulk:
There are none so dactylic as Gronsky & Skulk!

She put it in his backpack.

ELEVEN

Another Trip

In April, he was dressed as — believe it or not — Mother Earth for Earth Day Month: a reddish-blond Afro (representing the sun? Ronald McDonald?), and a genuine National Geographic globe costume, with major geographical features appliqué. On his feet, for some submerged reason, flippers. On the speakers, an adaptation of selections from Genesis, Chapter 1, King James version. You don't want to hear it.

What did they know, Gronsky & Skulk? They were as far from understanding how to work the world as Bouvard & Pécuchet, as far from the reins of control as Vladimir & Estragon, perhaps as doomed as Clyde & Bonnie. They knew only that they needed help to bring about their Teaching Moment, whatever it was.

But, as the old German saying has it, *Wenn die Not am höchsten, ist die Rettung am nächsten* — when the need is greatest, rescue is closest at hand. As they were making their April Santa-sighting, there was Jodi McClain again. Did she <u>live</u> at Kaufmann's?

"Oh, hi, Dr. Gronsky!"

Bubbly as ever, for Teresa even more irritatingly so, as Jodi was decked out in her spring teenager look, blond hair in double pigtails, shortish plaid skirt, knee socks and Birkies. Better sluttish, her rival thought. But the feeling was anything but mutual:

"And hi, Ms. Skulkington!"

("She remembered my name!")

"Dr. Gronsky told me you were working on a book to respond to *What's The Matter With Kansas?* I met a really interesting man the other day out in Cullison, and you might want to interview him. Mr. Libby — like Scooter Libby? — ask anyone in town."

"Libby... Cullison. Isn't that the right-wing sculptor whacko Frank talks about in the book?"

"Well, that's why I'm recommending you go see him. You might be surprised."

"Aha!" T.L. jumped on the hint. "You mean he's not what Frank suggests?"

"See what you think," Jodi said. "Sorry, gotta run. Got a heavy date tonight. It was great seeing you again, Ms. Skulkington." And out she went, into the uncertain glory of a Kansas April day.

Needless to say, the two scholars hied it right home to check the text. Richard recalled that Pratt county, a decade ago, had actually voted to secede from Kansas, and was hot to go. Teresa was a little put off by Frank's descriptions in the book. Her new left-for-right exchange might be hard-tested by a guy like J.B. Libby. Nevertheless, the chance to jump on Frank, if that was what Jodi was hinting at, still fired her combative personality, Love-the-One-Thing-the-Holy-Thing aside. She, too, was rarin' to go.

What a glorious day for a first motorcycle trip of the season, two and a half hours west, out into the prairie! CULLISON read the water tower, the only structure seriously assaulting the skyline of the tiny town. Its claims to fame were two: the world's deepest hand-dug well, and what the Cullison website (!) describes as "a bizarre collection of what is best described as 'kinetic art'. Wind powered objects that twirl and dance."

Never was euphemism more evasive. For stretching half a mile along Hwy 400 was a roadside display of visionary ferocity. A swastika made into a running man. A goat's skull over the words "PRESIDENT GINGRICH". Meaning? A sign concerning "Semen Clinton", and a boat, the USS KARL MARX over its dog bone-shaped caption, DOWN SHE GOES. Weathervanes, cast-iron birds, ghosts. The Main Stream Media labeled POLLUTED WITH LIBERAL VOMIT, one-way and street signs pointing in every direction.

An uncertain, ramshackle barn, extended with miscellaneous sheds right out of Al Capp's Dogpatch, now sheltered a menagerie of farm machinery long-unused. Over the entrance: KANZA

ART STUDIO. The BSA zoomed into the yard, and Richard searched for a stray piece of wood to keep the kickstand from sinking into the mud. There were plenty to be found.

They knocked, then poked their heads into a small front door leading into the mudroom of the structure.

"Hello?" Richard inquired.

No answer.

"Hello?" he yelled in.

Still nothing. A young woman, perhaps 14 or 15, came out from a small shed to the side of the barn.

"Looking for something?" she asked.

"Is Mr. Libby around?" Richard responded.

"Nope. Gone to the sell. Down to Pratt."

"You expect him soon?"

"What time is it?"

Richard consulted his new Casio, a gift from Terry to replace his outlandish pocket Ben.

"11:43. Damn! I promised never to do that!"

"What?" asked the girl.

"Give someone the time down to the minute. Now that I'm digital. I mean what's wrong with 'a quarter to twelve'"?

"Nothin'. But you shouldn't take the Lord's name in vain."

"You mean saying 'Damn!'?"

"You said it again."

Terry thought she'd better intervene in what could become an Abbot & Costello routine.

"We were looking for Mr. Libby," she said.

"Dad'll be back around noon, he said."

"Ah," Terry replied. "So you must be his daughter. I'm Teresa, and this is my partner, Richard."

"Your husband?"

"Yes." Why make trouble?, Terry thought.

"Whyn't you call him that, then?"

"Because in this case, he's my partner on a book we're writing — about interesting people in Kansas. I hear your Dad's a marvelous person."

"You think so?"

"We'd love to meet him."

"What makes you think he's marvelous? You read that book about what's wrong with Kansas?"

"Yes," Richard said, "as a matter of fact... "

"Yes," Teresa took over, "and that's what brought us out here. From Wichita."

"You want to interview him?"

"Well... yes, if he doesn't mind. For our book."

"I don't know if he'll mind."

"Can we wait for him — to ask?"

"Sure. Why not? C'mon in the shed and sit down."

Terry and Richard followed her into the ten by twelve shack, and closed the door behind them. The room was warm and aromatic. They sat down on the two rickety chairs, while the girl stirred a pot over a camp stove.

"This here's the world-famous Godsmell factory." Her guests were somewhat embarrassed that they were unaware of its existence.

"Oh?"

"Yup. You know all those Godsmell candles? The candles 'with the smell of Jesus'? I make 'em right here. Right in this room."

And indeed, with a moment's consideration, the room did seem a production facility, the walls lined with blocks of paraffin, and boxes of glass containers, the few shelves filled with stoppered brown bottles, and the remaining space stacked with small packing boxes. Teresa drew on her well-honed, if rarely used, social skills.

"I'm ashamed to say that Richard and I haven't heard about them. Can you tell us more — maybe for the book?"

"Oh. Sure. The recipe is sort of right in the Bible — Psalm 45:8. Myrrh, aloes, and cassia. You have to play around with the proportions, but I think I got it down now. At least a lot of people seem to like it. I sell a hundred cases every couple of weeks."

"Really?" Terry asked. The girl was pouring hot wax from the pot into a row of glass jars on the table. "How many candles in a case?"

"A dozen." She began inserting wicks into the thickening, fragrant brew.

"Twelve hundred candles every two weeks out of that little — well, medium size — pot? Why don't you use something bigger?"

"Can't. Couldn't handle it. Couldn't pour much more and still get the wicks in in time."

"Must be a lot of work," Richard observed.

"Yup. It's my ministry. To give people the fragrance of Christ, the oil of gladness, the reward of righteousness. They make for a very spatial experience. Want to help? Can you stick these labels on while I pour the rest of this batch?"

Teresa took a tiny digital recorder from her leather jacket. "Could I ask you some questions, like for the book? Would you mind if I recorded your answers?"

"I thought you was here to talk to Dad."

"Well, we'll talk to him when he comes."

"OK. Sure. Fire away."

Teresa turned on the machine.

"First tell us your name."

"Bonnie Ann Libby."

"Thanks. Now, Bonnie... "

"Bonnie Ann. With no E."

"Bonnie Ann, as a 14-year Kansas girl, what... "

"Fifteen. Fifteen last October."

"As a 15-year old Kansas girl, what are your thoughts on the country right now?"

"You mean this whole country? America?"

"Yes."

"Um, I think God's watchin over us and that he's really protectin us. My heart's settled about the war especially. I think Bush is in control and he's a godly man."

A truck roared into the yard, and pulled its brake.

"That must be Dad now. You probably want to talk to him. He'll be wondering about the motorcycle."

"OK. One quick last question, all right?"

Bonnie Ann nodded.

"As a young, attractive girl... "

"Thank you, m'am."

"... do you have any thoughts about abortion?"

"God states it in the Bible very clearly that, you know, no killing. It's one of the ten commandments. That's killing."

A grizzled, older man poked his head in the door.

"You folks here for candles?"

"Uh... no, actually. Are you Mr. Libby?"

"That's me."

Bonnie Ann stepped in to ease the juncture.

"Daddy, this is Richard and Teresa, his wife, and they're from Wichita, and they're writing a book about interesting Kansas people, and they'd like to interview you."

"If you're willing," Richard offered.

"I'm bout as interestin' as they come around here, so come into the shop. I got work to do. You all finished with them, Bonnie Ann?"

"Yes. Very nice to meet you Sir, Ma'am. Want to buy a candle before you go off with Dad?"

"Sure/Of course" Richard and Terry said simultaneously. "How much?" he asked.

"$5.95 plus tax. That's 30¢. So $6.25."

She fetched a finished candle from an open carton. The label was beautifully lettered in italic, and featured a Rouault face of Christ. Richard and Terry glanced at one another in astonishment.

"Nice label!" she exclaimed. "Where'd you get that picture?"

"Cut it out of a magazine. They put it on the label at the printer. I like it. You can sort of see the smell."

She took change for a twenty out of a cigar box."

"Come on, if you're comin'. I gotta get to work."

They walked their boots through the mud into J.B. Libby's shop, a large, cold, room filled with welding equipment, power saws, tool boxes, wheelbarrows, cement mixers, an old tractor, half-scavenged, and heaps of miscellaneous junk. On the walls, hanging on 16-penny nails were rows and rows of cups. The sculptor peeled off his jacket and switched on a roaring space heater. He stood there in his sweatshirt and Carhartts, and faced his interlocutors.

"I suppose you read about me in Tom Frank's book?"

They nodded.

"Well, he didn't get a lot of things right — among them, I have the world's largest cup collection, probably ten thousand. Hell, I don't know why I got it, I just got it."

"Have you drunk a cup of coffee out of each one of them?" Richard joked, trying to make his subject — or perhaps himself — feel comfortable.

"Sheeit. Man, you're crazy."

"Your daughter wouldn't like that language, I bet."

"Well, hell, <u>she's</u> crazy — with all that smellygod stuff. Crazy as a loon. Like her mother."

"Where is her mother?" asked Teresa.

"Dead. Killed herself. Probably for the Lord."

"Oh, sorry to hear that."

"Thank you, M'am."

"Would you mind if I recorded some of what you say?" Terry asked.

She showed her recorder.

"On that little thing? I'll probably bust it."

"It's you against Sony."

"Japs? They don't stand a chance. So... " He points to the mike. "So can you allow swearing on this?"

"Absolutely. Swear to tell the truth, the whole truth, and nothing but the truth," Richard challenged.

"Awwwwright!"

"So, let's see," Teresa said, "What do you think of today's political situation?"

"Politicians from the top to the bottom are basically the same. The worst one is this asshole we got in there as president."

This was more surprising than Rouault.

"It took us two hundred and however many years it is," Libby continued, "but we finally got us an asshole. A genuine, thoroughbred asshole. It's enough to make a man puke up his soul. Example: this war in Iraq. I am so dead-set agin it. What goddam business we got over there? Into a foreign country that's none of our business, tryin to change a culture that is thousands of years before our time — and we're trying to change it? We're NOT going to change it. It's like tryin' to put socks on an octopus."

"So you don't agree with the way we're taking all the money from this country and sending it over there to spend on the war?"

"Well, yeah, well, um. They're bitchin about free medicine. Well for God's sake the kind of money we're spendin over there, you could give everybody free medicine. And a good American truck, too."

"What do most people in town think?"

"Well sheeeit. They sure don't like me."

"And?"

"Well, hell, that's their problem, not mine. Only reason I do all this sculpture, these signs, is to piss people off."

"And does it work?"

"Oh God, yeah. Like a whore in St. Louis."

"This is a pretty religious area, isn't it?" Richard chimed in.

"Yeah, well, rednecks. But you know, some of these guys get a half a million dollars — a year!"

"For what?

"For nothin'. For sittin' around doin' nothin'. Farm welfare, I call it. They call it 'subsidy' a course. But go down to this goddam cafe, these old farmers — I'm not agin' 'em. But they'll go down to the goddam cafe, and they'll set over in the corner, and they get their goddam welfare checks for a hundred and fifty thousand dollars a year, and they'll bitch about some woman gettin — what is it? — aid to dependent children, and she might get a couple of hundred dollars a month, and her kids get free lunch, and them sonsabitches bitch about that!"

"You were written up in this Tom Frank's book, but you know, you're not anything like what he wrote," Teresa said.

"Well, sure! But who gives a shit? I don't care."

It went like that for half an hour, denunciations of the entire political scene, left and right, while J.B. Libby torched his way around a quarter-inch sheet of scrap iron, and painted its sign,

MISSION ACCOMPLISHED. It was a Jewish star whose intersecting triangles were made up of sprawled dead bodies.
"Like it?" he asked.
"Are those dead Palestinians, or dead Israelis?"
"Six a one, half dozen a the other," he said cryptically.
"OK," Teresa said, "One last question."
"Shoot."
"What do you think about 9/11?"
"Fuckin ragheads — what do you expect? It's just like here with this religious stuff — a total crock a shit. And you can quote me."

On the ride home, they calculated that, given, say, a 50% markup over expenses, Bonnie Ann must net almost $2,000 a week from her Godsmells.
"What do you think she does with all that?" Teresa screamed in Richard's ear.
"I don't know," he yelled back. "Give it to the church?"
"What church?" was the answer.
Another shouted conversation:
"If even Libby buys the 9/11 story, what chance do we have of convincing normal people?" Richard yelled.
"Yeah," she bellowed back. "Maybe we should try to think of something else."
And finally, her last observation, yelled into his right ear:
"See? I told you Frank was full of baloney."
At 80 mph, what could he say? They took in the late afternoon skyscape till they hit Wichita.

All right, so maybe Jodi's help in finding a Teaching Moment was a red herring. But so is most help.

TWELVE

Prairie Fire 2

3 May, 2006

My Dear Children,

   I must adjure you not to judge too quickly; the Father and the Daughter are not at odds with one another. Both embrace the Truth, and the Truth embraces them — he the body and she the spirit. Your prophetic vision must engage all aspects of humanity — the vaster and eternal aspects of the human soul, along with all its kinks and prejudices, its selfishness and jealousy and small dishonesties. Love them all, and try to bring into your fold even the mis–births of heaven and the jettisons from hell.
   For your task is huge. The new slavery of mind and soul is the sum of all villainies, a potential death sentence for America. Men now are of rigid mold — servile, dog-like to the powerful. The Free State of Kansas will change all that — if you can wisely act.
   You must know that so deep-seated and radical a disease demands fierce action. The condition now besotting all leaves men coarse and women shallow. The government carnival of crime and rapine is a disgrace to civilization. But such a vision of the damned may still stir the world. A mighty struggle is gathering around you — the greatest moral war — "To loose the bands of wickedness, to undo the heavy burdens, and to let the oppressed go free, and that ye break every yoke..." My children, to recognize an evil and not strike it down is sinful. Nature is mourning for its afflicted children, and hung be the Heavens in scarlet! For this, we are all held accountable by God, for a cause in which every man, woman, and child of the entire human family has a deep and awful interest. Isaiah warns us — Woe unto them that call evil good; and good evil; that put darkness for light, and light for darkness.

You are both gentle people, as am I. But there may again come a time — and it has likely come already — in which there must be force and blood to make true war on slavery. You two must strike a blow which will arouse the country and shake it to the foundations. You know how dear life is to you, and how dear life is to your friends. And remembering that, consider that the lives of others are as dear to them as yours are to you. Do not, therefore, take the life of anyone if you can possibly avoid it, but if it is necessary to take life, then you must be ready to make sure work of it.

God has chosen you as an instrument in His war for freedom. Cry aloud, and spare not, Isaiah tells us, Lift up thy voice like a trumpet, and show the people their trans–gression, and their sins. But the crimes of this guilty land may never be purged away except with blood. Without the shedding of blood, there is no remission of sins. A few men slain now may save millions of innocents later. That's how terror, in the hands of the righteous, works.

I share with you an incident of my youth, one that made the very greatest impression upon me. Through childish imprudence, I had lost some small funds my father had lent me. He judged I should be punished, and my plan was to recompense my pittance as reckoned in strokes from a blue-beach switch, laid on masterly. When the debt was half-paid, to my utter astonishment, Father stripped off his shirt and seating himself on a block gave me the whip and bade me lay it on to his bare back. I dared not refuse to obey, but at first I did not strike hard. "Harder," he said, "Harder, harder!" until he received the balance of my account. Small drops of blood showed on his back where the tip end of the tingling beach cut through. This was my first practical lesson in the doctrine of the atonement. Consider it well.

Richard and Teresa, you will have to gather the forces for your struggle. You will want industrious, not gassy, men to work with, men agile, alert and audacious. Some such conspiracy is needed for the purpose of insurrection. But let them be capable of shedding blood. No kittenish weaklings, no mild-mannered Unitarians, no cowards who prefer peace with the slavers to war. And no men whose courage depends on whisky. You want temperance men, and you, too, must put by your vices. You must be Christians, true soldiers of the Lord. Avoid any business which would prevent you from answering His call. Be ready to always wind up your affairs and obey. Armored by God, you must be free to go forth to smite his enemies down.

You will want always to justify your acts, for many will see you as fanatics, guilty of a great wrong against God and humanity and would feel themselves perfectly right to interfere. You will be outlaws, with bounties on your heads.. Though you do not love warfare but peace, and act only in obedience to the will of the Lord and for His children's' sake, you will be hunted pursued as if you served only the Devil. Therefore, do seek out <u>now</u> some hidden refuge in which you may be safe. Be prepared.

But above all, courage, courage, courage. The unseen Hand that guideth you and who hath indeed held thy right hand, may hold it still, though you may not have known Him at all as you ought. Courage for what may come. Be not afraid.

Your friend,
Osawatomie Brown

THIRTEEN

Stalking Santa

On the fourth of May, he was Zapata, or someone very like. The muzak cycled some mariachi ditty whose *palabras* G&S couldn't catch, and the children fondled the 9 mm bullets (real?) in his cartridge belt.

So tantalized, curious, frustrated and determined were they, that Richard and T.L. returned two days later for further inspection. By then he was a passable Mrs. Santa — or more likely Mother Santa-*en-vacances* — for the loudspeakers featured some Sinatra clone crooning *M is for the moccasins she gave me...* , and on through the acronym, outfits, tees, hats, electronics, raincoats — to the apotheosis: *Put them all together, they spell MO-THER, the word that means the world to me.*

Male, female; fat, thin; black, white and brown. Who was this Man With A Thousand Faces, and what did he portend? Why, even, did they <u>think</u> he portended anything for them, and for The Teaching Moment for The Kause? They just did: they knew it.

So how to find out? They couldn't share their plans with him. Too inchoate. Not even plans. Besides, what if he were a rightwinger, a Frankian Kansan who would patriotically rat on them? What if he were indiscreet — or nuts? No, they had to find out more about this guy before proceeding in his direction. But how?

"We could spy on him," said T.L.. "Find out where he lives, where he goes when he's not here."

"You free this afternoon?" her partner asked.

"Yup."

"Me, too," he said. "So let's just do it."

And they did.

"What are Santa's hours?" they asked a sales associate in jewelry. Hi, My Name Is Deb.

"You mean Mother Santa?" Deb asked in return.

It wasn't clear if this was a company line, or if she really <u>believed</u> he was Mother Santa.

"Yes. Mother Santa."

"Eight to four-thirty Monday through Thursday, ten to six-thirty Friday and Saturday, Sundays noon to five. Mondays off."

It was already four. They would browse for half an hour, then begin their tail.

At 4:30 precisely, Mother Santa gently lifted the last child from her red-skirted lap, walked down off the stage, and exited through a door marked "Employees Only". They waited for her — him — to come back out. They felt they would recognize him.

4:45, 5:00. Only three clearly teen-age associates had come through. How long could it take her — him — to change? Could one of the clearly teen-age associates have been... ? No. Different sizes, different builds. But could they? 5:10. Wait a minute. What if there's a back door out of the dressing room, through the shipping area or something? Damn! Stupid, stupid, stupid. There were two of them. One could have covered... But how would one communicate contact to the other without losing him? They didn't own cell phones. And by the time she would run in from the street to tell him, he'd be gone. Besides, she'd likely attract his attention by running. And vice versa, Rich to T.L.. Though there <u>was</u> a chance that he, inside, could follow Santa outside, and signal her — provided the back door was in sight of the front door — which it wasn't likely to be. No. They would need some tools. Like walkie-talkies. They spent dinner time at Radio Shack. "*You've got questions. We've got answers*," was the RS motto.

Isn't modern technology wonderful? For twenty bucks plus tax they walked away with a set of two 22-channel GMRS/FRS 2-way radios with a three mile range. Low end, but it should work for a hundred yards, max.

But they also walked away with visions of spy-ware sugar-plums dancing in their heads. Hey, for only $379, they could invest in a supersensitive, long-range amplified shotgun microphone with digital headphones, and listen into his conversations with the children from some hiding place on the mezzanine. Cheaper, though, to bug his throne — only $57.95. If they had to.

But for now, walkie-talkies, real ones far better than the toys they each had as kids, and for a similar price. They returned to Kaufmann's to check the location and staff use of back exits.

There were two, one at each end of the building, both leading out into a service alley running parallel to Douglas. There was also a loading dock with its own associated exit. But all were visible to the same observer. There were of course, side customer entrances and exits, but they could be seen by the team member inside. Teresa went into the store while Richard remained in the alley.

"Can you hear me?" the shrill voice seemed to shout from out of the box.

"Yes, I can, yes," he answered. "You don't have to shout!"

"<u>You</u> don't have to shout," the voice replied.

They both turned down the volume to a more clandestine level.

The next evening, they were properly posted. And there he was at 4:50, coming back into the store from the door beside the stage. T.L. was sure. It <u>had</u> to be him. Maybe. Richard was to pick them up at the Broadway exit.

Santa walked to the bus stop on the next block. Ah, good. He takes a bus home. They also stood there, boarded the 14 with him when it came along, and got off — with him and many others — at the University Plaza stop. Good again. Richard's home turf. On to the WSU box office at Duerksen where they watched him buy a ticket for something. But what they didn't know.

"Shall we ask them what he bought?" Richard whispered.

"No. Too obvious. Unless the guy in the booth is one of your students."

"No."

Santa turned to leave the building and, noticing them in the lobby, nodded politely as he went by. Too suspicious to just leave and follow him. So enough tailing for today. The system works.

But what did he buy tickets for? They scanned the posters around the room. A Shockers game? Maybe. The Jazz concert at Miller? Could be. No. They both hit on it at the same time:

THE WICH!
A Student Opera Workshop adaptation of
Humperdinck's Hansel & Gretel,
with a post-9/11 attitude!
One weekend only.

Good graphic, too. Margaret Hamilton flying her broomstick through the smoking ruins of the World Trade Center.

That's it, surely. Hansel & Gretel. Little children. He <u>loves</u> little children — presumably. Or maybe he's sick of them. And the "post-9/11" stuff — If he's interested in that... .

Up to the window they went. Sunday was the night Santa got off early, so they chose that, got their tickets, and bussed back to the BSA still parked at the store.

But The Wich was a month away: Much work could be done in the interim — if he was there at all, alone or accompanied. And the great American Clock of Affective Historical Amnesia was ticking.

Did they need more tools? Maybe. What <u>about</u> that Radio Shack Bionic Ear? Less than four-hundred bucks — wasn't the Kause worth that more-or-less trivial investment? But they couldn't be sure he was the one, <u>the</u> one, to help them. And would listening in on his conversations with the children really yield critical information concerning the question? Throne bugging <u>was</u> cheaper. And maybe a bug or a spike-mike into the locker room would be even more productive? Say with a digital recorder...

Teresa suggested accosting him as a prostitute, wearing a wire, and getting him to open up before she did. Besides, if he were married, or even gay, they could maybe use the encounter as blackmail to force his cooperation. Richard nixed the plan. They would start by just following him home, unobtrusively, and take it from there.

On Project Day 2, they picked him up at the stage door, so to speak, and trailed him up Broadway to Barnes & Noble, back into the fiction section — P — but didn't dare enter the same aisle.

They watched through cracks in the shelves, browsing McCullers, Melville, Michener, Mishima, Musil, and Nabokov until Santa had made his selection and left for the registers.

"OK, let's not lose him this time," Teresa whispered (though he couldn't have heard her).

"Wait," Richard said, "Let's first see what he bought. I saw exactly where he was, and what level he got it from."

So they detoured around to the Ps, and there it was — a gaping hole on the shelf of the new Proust translations — one of the three volume twos, *In the Shadows of Young Girls in Flower.*

"Aha!," exclaimed Richard.

"Aha what?"

"Aha, he's reading Proust."

"So?"

"So maybe he is gay."

"You don't have to be gay to read Proust," Teresa observed. Young girls in flower?

"True," he admitted.

"Besides, if he were gay, he'd have bought *Sodom and Gomorrah*."

"You've read it?"

"Of course, what do you think I am, dumb?"

"The whole thing?"

"Seven volumes."

"I haven't," he admitted.

"That's obvious," she said.

"But he could be gay and just have not gotten to volume four yet."

"C'mon asshole, we're going to lose him again."

And they had. At the registers, he was nowhere to be seen. They searched the store, thinking he may have gone browsing elsewhere. No.

"Damn! One of us should have watched the registers while the other looked around."

"Dumb and dumber," Teresa agreed. "Bouvard & Pécuchet have nothing on us."

As with her poem, he didn't ask. One evidence of illiteracy was enough for the day. He <u>was</u>, after all, a professor. Granted, not a literature professor, but still...

Project Day 3 was more successful. They picked him up alleywise again, and walked behind him, she in the lead on the other side of the street, Richard ipsilateral, well enough behind to feel invisible, though Wichita streets are straight as truth. A nice day it was, and so, a long walk home — all the way down to Oliver and 31st.

Or at least they thought it was home. They saw him disappear into an old, four-story apartment house with an oddly elaborate courtyard with a fountain out of the Arabian Nights. "THE BAGHDAD," said the sign. The garden must have been the green zone. They prowled the garden and found a building entrance at each of its four corners. Which one he had used was unknown. But still, it was progress. And Gronsky thought she made a pretty sexy spy.

So he proposed an early morning stakeout. They could sit in the Chevy and pretend to neck for passersby. From the street, the back two courtyard entrances were visible, if not the front ones, facing in. 50% chance they could catch which one he came out of. And if not, they'd have cut the other possibilities down to two, and they'd cross that bridge when and if.

"Ridiculous," she said. "Where does that get us, even if we know which building he lives in? There are — what? — twenty, thirty mailboxes in each? And besides, where would we pee, if we had to?"

"You're right," he agreed. "We actually need to know what he <u>thinks</u>, not where he lives. We could interview his neighbors, though... "

Gronsky & Skulk were not making much progress.

"Hey, how about a trash survey?" she suggested. "We find out the trash pick-up day and check out the dumpster the night before."

"How would we tell his stuff from everyone else's?"

"Yeah, that could be a problem," she allowed. "But still, if we went through everything... "

"Too much work. Too much guesswork. We've been doing ok tailing him. Let's keep that up and see what we can learn."

So they did. They picked him up on Project Day 4, and applied a loose tail, both wearing dark colors. Unfortunately, the day was quite bright, and they may have been conspicuous. They lost him quickly. Or did he lose them?

He did seem more cautious. He would check the alley both ways before emerging. PD 7 was revealing: he left the building from the front and walked to a late-model Lexus parked nearby. Aha! A Lexus! Where does a department store Santa get the money for a Lexus? Very suspicious. Gronsky & Skulk noted the license number, and next day staked it out at closing time — binoculars from the BSA. And there he was. The Lexus headed up Broadway, right on Lincoln, and on east toward 135. They tried to stay in his blind spot, but he made a left on a changing red, and they were stuck two cars behind. They picked him up again several blocks down, he himself slowed by traffic and they with motorcycle freedom on the right. He made another left, and they cut through a fortuitous Gulf station to avoid the light. Then he made four successive right turns, speeding up and slowing down, and they were forced into a too-obvious imitative pattern. Perhaps this jig was up. Just after the last right, he parked, and as they shot on past him, they were too shame-faced to pull a U and follow on foot. This guy was a pro. Pro what?

Their next try was all-too convincing. This time the Lexus led them on a merry early-evening chase north on 135, barreling towards Salina. They were both in the left lane, Gronsky & Skulk two SUVs back. Suddenly, without signaling, like a quarterback finding a hole, the Lexus swerved through a small break in the right-lane traffic, and zipped out exit 33, leaving his pursuers walled off in the left lane, assigned, alas, to exit 34 or beyond. Fun and games. He was surely on to them — at least to the couple on the BSA. But they knew that. Maybe they should start using the Chevy.

But Hansel & Gretel, or rather, The Wich, was coming up in ten days, and they'd see what that would bring. <u>If</u> they'd guessed the right performance, <u>and</u> if he were there.

FOURTEEN

The Wich

Wilner Auditorium was packed to the gills. Why? Did the students confuse <u>this</u> Engelbert Humperdinck with the crooner of "Let There Be Love"? Hard to believe, but anything is possible in academia. But there they were, with notebooks in hand. Ah! Probably class assignments. Music appreciation? Cultural Studies?

It may have been Cultural Cool, though, communicated by word of mouth and bush telegraph. For the pit was filling not with the usual long-dressed and snazzily tuxedo'd crew of musicians, but with something out of Columbine/South Central — black clothes and torn, ringed, spiked and razorbladed, instruments at the ready. An adaptation with an attitude, indeed.

In the huge crowd, and from their balcony seats, Santa was nowhere to be seen. Perhaps he was sitting beneath them at the rear of the orchestra. Perhaps he was not there at all. They'd check at intermission.

But wait — there <u>was</u> no intermission. "The performance will be in one act something like one hour. The hour which is at hand." Hmm. All right. They'd try to catch him at the end, before he left the theater.

An A was given by the oboe, and standard tuning went on.

"At least the attitude doesn't seem to affect tuning," Richard offered hopefully.

The lights dimmed, and on the scrim in front of them flashed the following message. THERE WILL BE NO ANNOUNCEMENT THANKING THE WICHITA SAVINGS BANK FOR ITS SUPPORT. FOR AS BERTOLT BRECHT OBSERVED: "WHAT IS THE ROBBING OF A BANK COMPARED TO THE FOUNDING OF ONE?"

"Phew. Heavy duty," T.L. remarked. "What would Daddy say?"

The student conductor made his way to the podium to great applause and whooping. He faced his audience and raised a clenched fist.

"They must know something we don't," Teresa said. "Who is that? The Shockers quarterback?"

Richard shrugged.

"Dunno. Never heard of him."

"You don't get the most with-it professor award, I guess," she said.

"So you want a divorce?"

She poked him in the ribs with her pointy elbow. The audience quieted for that magic moment in darkness, before it all began.

And begin it did, the famous overture, with a chorale of four-part horn sweetness, the "Now I Lay Me Down To Sleep" tune, known or unknown, of all our childhoods. On the scrim, DAWN OVER WICHITA, 12-hours misplaced, or perhaps the advertised "attitude", a sarcastic comment on the sleepwalking days of Kansans. In any case, what a gorgeous opening: the famous *Abendsegen*, or evening prayer, sweet, sweet — but not sugary-so. Rather sweetly rich and creamy, like premium chocolate, or a cantaloupe at maximum bouquet, an aural caress. The projected sunrise was lovely too, the gleaming river, the Hyatt Regency with its sparkling waterfall. THE BIRDS GREET THE SUN, says the scrim, and the great Kansan sky becomes slowly filled with birds, a gentle nature film, like PBS. As the overture builds with Wagnerian harmonies, the birds become more intense — wait! — there's a flying birds shot from *Duck Soup*, couldn't be, I must have imagined it. The Meistersingerish counterpoint thickens, as does the sky, and my God! it's the title bird-melee from Hitchcock, wait! was it really? I thought I... and the flocks fly north — could that be Margaret Hamilton on her broom in among them?? — as the camera pans lyrically eastward over the city towards the wrong side of Wichita's tracks, the music lusciously Wagner-without-Nazism. Sunrise over slums is <u>also</u> beautiful — as long as you're in long-shot. But the overture winds down, gently, strangely chromatic, again calling forth the *Abendsegen* — a prayer, however twisted — as the camera climbs a filthy stairway to an attic apartment. The scrim rises on the opening scene.

"That was something," Teresa said.

Richard could only nod his head.

SCENE ONE: CHILDREN AT PLAY read the sign, flown in from above, courtesy, Richard thought, of the Brecht-groupies, all males of which wore Bertolt haircuts, granny glasses, and blue workshirts with ties.

The set was impressive, a German-expressionist hovel of Dickensian poverty, scant of furniture, mattresses on floor, wash hanging criss-cross throughout the room. The children, one supposes, are Hänsel and Gretel, but they are dark, far from the blond, cherubic Hummelkinder usually depicted, dark-haired, dark-complexioned, and in rags. As the sister tries to teach the crippled brother to dance, she sings,

Amahl, come and dance with me,
Both my hands I offer thee...

And the brother responds,

Hanan, you must show me now,
Dance I would if I knew how...

And she shows him.

Right foot first, left foot then
Round about, and back again.

All right, Amahl and Hanan — OK. *Hänsel and Gretel* doesn't have to be about Hänsel and Gretel in postmodernity, right? And after all, this isn't *Hänsel and Gretel*, it's *The Wich*, even if it's abducted Humperdinck along for the ride. So Amahl and Hanan, why not? And the dance is very charming, the children ducking in and out of the hanging wash, whacking the sheets with crutch for rhythm, and peeking out between the legs of long johns.

With your hands you clap, clap, clap
With your crutch you tap, tap, tap...

Très gai.

Flying quickly past a filthy window — Margaret Hamilton on her broom, accompanied by a flock of crows.

A woman bursts into the room, most likely their mother.

SCENE TWO, the flying sign informs us, POVERTY DOES NOT IMPROVE HUMAN CHARACTER, as Mom bursts into the room like a raging Valkyrie — and looking a lot like Miss Gulch.

"What's going on?" she demands,

You call this working, all this dancing and singing?

She is so mad that she knocks a jug of milk off onto the floor and all over her skirt. Milk was all there was for supper.

Out! Out! Get out! Find some food. Just wait till your father comes home.

She pushes them out the door, and breaks down weeping.

"I'm dead tired, dead, dead... God, dear God, send some money! Lots of money!"

Footsteps on the stairs. A ragged voice singing an oddly jocular tune.

Brecht was of the opinion that music was strongest when it opposed the text. Happiness is best set off by a dirge, and sadness by a gay tune. Contrast heightens.

But here, it wasn't the Brecht groupies responsible. Humperdinck himself sets a most nasty text to gay tralalas.

BALLAD OF THE EMPTY STOMACH
Basic lifestyle of those needing:
Every day there's little feeding,
Ain't no money in the till
And the belly's emptier still.
Tralalala, tralalala
Eating would be best by far!

On and on, verse after sardonic verse of class struggle, his wife watching, and plotting her solution.

The cupboard bare
The cellar bare,
And in the belly,
Wild beasts there!
Tralalala.

She stands, and cuts him off. Oh Lordy, Engelbert, stop thine ears! It's the True-To-Grimm-Anti-Disneyfication-Lobby, getting real. No more the "Oh dear, I was overwrought, and now you say there's a witch out there, let's go find the children right away" mother. No, here in this production with an attitude, the original Grimm tale is reasserted, and to the ominous witch music, the mother sings her plan and exhortations:

The children must be done away with
Lest all of us do starve to death.

A lifeboat strategy, cruel, but rational in its way. It is better that <u>some</u> survive if not all can. If we parents die, she argues, so will the children, unable to support themselves. If they die, well... we can likely make it, and have more. When Father demurs,

The poor, poor children...

she sings grim words to the strains of Alberich's curse:

Well then, you fool,
Get out your tools
To hammer together four coffins!

What can Father say? Only this:

At least, let's find them, <u>then</u> decide
We might make some dough if we let <u>them</u> provide,
And have them send their wages.

Too emotionally exhausted to argue, Mother agrees, and off they go to recoup and assess their chattel.

"I'm afraid that's how the real story goes," Richard whispered.

"You're telling me? It was one of Daddy's favorites for bedtime story. Part of our moral education. Family structure and investment, don't ya know. I prefer condoms."

"I don't."

What did he mean?

The scrim drops down with the title SCENE THREE: IN THE JUNGLE OF CITIES, as the children trudge in silhouette through scenes of their own slum neighborhood and the more covert slumscape of downtown, dumpster diving along the way. Night is falling, things grow dark. Hanan is frightened; Amahl is brave. And then, pitch blackness.

Hanan, I cannot find the way!

CHILDREN IN NIGHTTOWN

As the audience's eyes accommodate, shadowy shapes are barely seen, performing shadowy deeds. A hugely-hatted figure approaches the children, offers them something soporific — for they put it in their mouths, then curl up in each other's arms to sleep. A very faint image of the Oz-poppy scene fills the scrim as the Sandman sings his aria in the gloom. He loves the children, he says, and watches over them, and sends them mantic dreams.

The scrim leaves 30s Hollywood, and transits dimly to the lived American life à la clique Artaud.

WHAT THE BUDDHA SEES

Over winsome cascades of Meistersinger melodies, once Humperdinck's pantomime of angels, what the Buddha sees now are current forms of old age, sickness and death — crowds and hunger, people armed, deformed and masked, prisoners, corpses, amputees; the retarded, the disfigured, the shattered. Humans laced in straight jackets; men with bagged heads, adorned with orange jumpsuits; dwellings bombed, children bulldozed, sadness, despair, and weeping and wailing; helicopters overhead.

Quel montage! Hänsel and Gretel's — or rather, Amahl and Hanan's dream. All to the most luminous of music.

The scrim rises on SCENE FOUR, the lights fade slowly up, THE WICH'S TOWERS are dimly seen in the rosy morning light, the Meistersinger music continues, glorious, the sunlight grows...

One tower seems an edible dwelling, with curtains, window boxes of flowers, gingerbready decorations. The other, less inviting, seems a kind of Rapunzel-prison, with barred windows, a massive gate, and attached to a large clay oven. The complex stands in a garbage-strewn lot littered with old mattresses and defunct major appliances. In their midst, incongruous, a jungle gym decorated with ribbons.

"Oh heavens," Amahl declares, "what is this wondrous place?"

*And what a scrumptious smell I smell
Of chocolate and cakes our hunger to quell...*

He pokes the tower eaves with his crutch: a piece of roof comes off and falls into his hands. He sniffs at it, and takes a bite.

*Oh, taste this, Hanan, sister mine,
There's nothing at all that tastes so fine!*

Hanan must find it luscious too, for she breaks off a small piece of shutter to sample. A flock of crows flies down and settles noisily on the jungle gym as the children gorge, making fair to demolish both towers.

From inside the house, a voice that might have been that of their own mother:

*Nibble, nibble, little mouse
Who's that nibbling at my house?*

They look at one another, astounded, confused. Hanan comes up with a tentative response:

*The breeze, the breeze
It's just that, if you please...*

Not too convincing.

The upper half of the house door opens and The Wich's head appears. She looks awfully like the Wicked Witch of the West, who looks awfully like Miss Gulch, who looks awfully like their mother. Most disconcerting. The Wich smiles winsomely.

*Two little angels, oh how sweet,
Such charming children* (to herself) *and good to eat!*

Amahl is not the most polite of children:

*Who <u>are</u> you, hag? — you look so awful!
We've not done anything unlawful.*

He hides the cake behind his back. The Wich seems insulted.

*I am Rosina — a worthy find.
I dearly cherish all mankind.
I'm innocent as children dear
Like you — that's why I'm glad you're here.*

Come in the house, dear little mice
And you'll find everything so nice...

The children make a break for it, but the Wich draws out her juniper wand, and freezes them in their tracks:

Hocus pocus, malus locus,
To run away, you needn't try!
Hocus pocus, bonus jocus
You can't escape my evil eye!

The crows fly off in all directions, screeching wildly, while The Wich ties Amahl up, locks him in her small Bastille, and tosses his crutch in among the heaps of garbage. Sensing her timid obedience, she disenchants Hanan with a wave of her wand, and sends her to gather wood for the oven. The fire is lit, and in a fit of joy over the upcoming meal she grabs her broom and rides wildly around the house, joined by the crows, by Margaret Hamilton and *Apocalypse Now* helicopters in rear projection, and shrieking out her Wich's song, in most frightening gestalt. Sensing the fire to be ready, she lands, and orders Hanan to inspect it. It's the old ploy:

"I am so slow
That I don't know
How to look in upon tiptoe.
Perhaps you don't know me —
I need you to show me...

While there may have been some eighteenth century witch who'd fallen for that, with its subsequent pushing-in, this savvy Wich was no fool. As Hanan is leaning in to show her how she doesn't know, the Wich runs up behind, and shoves the well-intentioned girl right in — and locks the oven door behind her. Hanan's screams are heard over Humperdinck's agitated music.

"I can't deal with this," Teresa told her partner. "It's too sick."

But she hain't seen nothin yet. This was a production with attitude.

The Wich fetches the zombied Amahl from the dungeon, lugging him — stiff as a board — under one arm. Into the oven with Number two, the better to bake them.

It's hard to know which displayed more attitude — The Wich's performance (to Humperdinck) of "Ding Dong, the Kids are Dead", or the arrival of the parents (SCENE FIVE: SAVED) who, with only slight hesitation, accept the situation, and sing the words of the resurrected gingerbread children of the original:

Saved are we
And freed forever...

while dancing with The Wich, their liberator. No doubt: poverty does not improve human character. They reprise "With your hands you clap, clap, clap", and the opera ends with lambent and twisting strains of the Evening Prayer. Though it is likely not yet evening.

After stunned silence, the applause was deafening — at least from the students. It <u>had</u> been a memorable performance. Gronsky & Skulk just sat there, depressed.

T.L. the Indomitable was the first to snap out of its spell.
"Hey — he may be escaping!"
"Who? Oh, yeah. We'd better get downstairs."
And there he was — or at least they thought it was he — heading out the door and toward the parking lot. They ran for the BSA, and waited across from the campus exit to the street. He waved as he turned, and drove leisurely off in the Lexus, with Gronsky & Skulk an irrelevant two cars behind him. But he didn't head home. Instead, he drove to the slum neighborhood of the show, parked, and walked quickly down the street, turning left into the first alley. They followed at thirty yards. When G&S turned the alley corner, they almost bumped noses with him — standing there facing them in the dark, his karate hands in his pockets.

"Can I help you?" he asked.
"Um, yes," Richard offered. "Uh... did you like the show? The Wich?"

Lame, but Santa took it in stride.

"Yes. Quite a bit."

The awkward ball was still in their court, as Santa looked them over. T.L. turned on the charm.

"Hi. I'm Terry Skulkington, and this is my partner, Richard Gronsky."

Her proffered hand pulled back, unshaken.

"You see, we..."

Richard jumped in. "We saw you take on those thieves at Kaufmann's back in, was it December? and we just wanted..."

What <u>did</u> they want? No one standing there knew, so the ellipsis just hung in the alley like...

"Yes?" inquired Santa, amused. The Skulkington Finishing School kicked in.

"We wanted to thank you, to tell you how much we admired your skill, and your modesty..."

"And also your acting ability, uh, the convincing character changes month to month..."

"And the costumes, the makeup. Very well done," she added.

"Very," Richard agreed.

The silence was dark, not golden.

"You <u>are</u> the man who plays Santa?" Teresa asked tentatively.

"Ho, ho, ho?" Richard detailed.

"Ho, ho, ho," Santa confirmed, mechanical, enigmatic.

"We'd love to talk with you a bit," Richard said.

"Yes," said hostess T. "Would you like to come by for a drink? Our place? It's right downtown."

"Three won't fit on your BSA," Santa coolly remarked.

"Uh, well, you can follow us. We'll give you a motorcycle escort!" the professor enthused, jocund.

More silence as Santa studied them. Their autonomic systems were unsure whether to blush or blanch, so they likely remained the same.

"All right," he said. "Lead the way."

They did.

They still didn't know his name.

FIFTEEN

Job Interview(s)

No-name Santa sat on the livingroom couch in his gray Armani suit, his thin legs crossed, his silk socks flashing darkly, a thin man, yes, but one exuding sleekness and power, an impression brought forth by his Mifune performance as Santa and since sustained.

He was by no means unpleasant-looking. Yet beyond his odd allurement, there reigned a kind of melancholy of... experience?... which gave his sky-blue eyes a whiff of endless night behind the day. His face was lean, almost hairless, and slightly pitted by acne. It seemed — in fact, his whole being seemed — as if it had been designed on an Etch-A-Sketch, all straight lines and right-tending angles, as if his very DNA might have been ladder-like, not helical. His hair was steely, without being gray, the hair of a man in his early or middle forties.

His skin was somewhat odd: leathery perhaps, with a gray tinge that might appear corpselike in bluish light, yet here, in the warm incandescence, emitted only a faint, metallic glow. There was a sharklike aspect to his image, which gave him something of the air of a submarine, a small one, pre-nuclear, yet deadly.

But his oddest feature was his ears — smallish, even rudimentary — appropriate to a beast that might want to cut through water.

Meticulous he seemed, alert, and practiced in something out of the ordinary. He smelled faintly of cologne.

"Drink?" Teresa asked.

Santa nodded.

"What'll you have?"

"Anything non-alcoholic," he offered.

"How's OJ?"

He nodded again. "OJ is fine, Ma'm." Slight, unnameable accent.

"Thank you," thought The Skulkington Finishing School. And "You're welcome."

Santa watched his hosts carefully with a gaze peculiar to people who don't want to be friendly.

Richard poured chablis for himself and Teresa while Teresa fetched the juice. He eyed the strange guest whose gray chilliness seemed to lower the temperature of the usually warm room, so filled with colorful books.

"There you go," said Teresa, handing him a large glass.

"Thank you, Ma'm" he said, and lowered the glass to his lap. He would drink very little.

In the wake of a theater evening, Richard could not help thinking "Iago," a character who, no matter how crowded the scene, stays locked inside himself, incommunicado.

The three were seated on couch and chair, around the coffee table, the hosts almost sorry they had initiated this.

"So," said Richard, with forced bonhomie, "I'm Richard Gronsky. I'm a history prof at the university, and this is Teresa Skulkington, my partner."

"Miles Hippie," responded their guest.

"Hm. What sort of a name is that?" Richard asked.

"If you prefer, I have others," said the man of many faces.

"Like?" Teresa asked, watching him as quizzically as he was watching them.

"That's enough for now," Miles Hippie returned. He noticed their disappointment. "If you don't like 'Mr. Hippie', you can call me Dr. Slop."

This was perhaps the oddest comment either of them had heard in their collective seven decades. Dr. Slop? 'Scientifick operator'? Male midwife? Midwife to what? Still, it was intriguing to a Yalie — if a hard prompting to follow.

"Mr. Hippie will do fine," she said.

"Fine for what?" he inquired coolly.

"You mean why did we ask you over?"

He nodded.

"Well/You see... " G&S attempted simultaneously. Teresa gave Richard the "after you" sign.

"We were impressed seeing you with those crooks at Christmas..."

"And by your acting ability," Teresa added. "So many convincing characters."

"And children are the best judge — you can't fake out children..."

"... very easily..."

They waited for a response. Some acknowledgement. None came.

"Well," Richard continued, "we just thought you might be able to help us with a little project..."

"And what is that?" Mr. Hippie asked.

"What do you think of today's political situation?" Teresa asked, thinking she might repeat her success with J.B. Libby.

Miles Hippie broke out in a huge laugh — that odd combination of seal bark and Santa-ish ho-ho-ho-ing they had remarked at Kaufmann's. Though surprising, and even frightening, it was by no means unpleasing, in contrast to his general severity.

"Who wants to know?" Mr. Hippie asked.

Richard leaned forward, elbows on knees.

"Let me lay our cards on the table."

"Always a good idea," Hippie observed, a remark which, in the context of his demeanor, was as curious as "Dr. Slop."

"Here's the thing," Richard continued. "This may sound crazy — initially.."

No visible reaction from the audience.

"... but we're trying to organize a movement to get Kansas to secede from the union..."

No reaction. Still that through-focused stare...

"You know, to create a new free state — as was imagined by the Free-Staters..."

"Back in the 1850's," Teresa added.

"But towards a different emancipation," Richard resumed, " — emancipation of the mind. The Free State of Kansas of the Mind. Something like that."

"Emancipation from what?" their guest inquired.

Here it was Richard that broke into laughter, though more deprecatory than seal-like.

"Take your pick!" he offered. "The whole kit and caboodle is up for grabs!"

"What do you think we might need emancipation from?" Teresa asked, intent on investigative probing.

"Well," Mr. Hippie offered, unexpectedly, "how about policing the world? Or group-think? Or shopping?"

Given Mr. Hippie's employer, this last was a surprise, but "Bingo!" both G&S thought. "He's with us. Cards on the table."

"So God is in the act of creating the world..." Mr. Hippie continued.

What was this guy about?

"...and darkness was upon the face of the deep. Like a tomb. And God said, 'Let there be light"; and there was light. Then God said, "Um... could I just see the darkness again?" And Hippie broke out in another huge laugh. Teresa and Richard looked at one another.

"I just thought you could use that story for your propaganda," their guest commented.

Perplexed, discombobulated, they laughed along with him. It was funny.

"All too true," Richard remarked. "So how do we make something better? That is the question. How do we get people to see that their light is... "

"Not necessarily preferable to darkness," Teresa construed.

"How?" Mr. Hippie inquired. "Do you have an answer?"

Richard stood up, and began his lecture-mode of pacing.

"We need to figure out a 'teaching moment' — something that will wake people up from their sleep, some event, some piece of news that can't be ignored, something that will reconfigure the way folks think about things... "

"Space aliens landing and giving a press conference." Mr. Hippie mused.

"Yes," Teresa affirmed. "Something like that. Some mind-blowing thing like that."

"Do you have any contact with space aliens?" Hippie inquired.

Was he serious?

"No. But we think we know something almost as shattering."

"Something that would blow open the whole scene, and make for vast new possibilities."

"And what might that be?" Mr. Hippie asked, apparently interested.

"Look," said Richard, "Americans seem to be able to forgive the government anything – phoney wars, stolen elections, giveaways to the rich, outsourcing jobs, loss of constitutional freedoms. Forgive or just be hoodwinked. Tom Franks wrote a book about..."

"I read it," Mr. Hippie noted.

"Well, great then — we're on the same page. But there's one thing Americans won't forgive."

"We think they won't forgive," T.L. noted.

"And that's any indication of government complicity in the 9/11 attacks. Any wide-spread suspicion, even."

"What makes you think so?"

"I... we don't know. It just seems beyond the bounds of what people will accept."

"Perhaps nothing is beyond the bounds."

"If that's the case..." T.L. threw up her hands.

"But we have to assume it's not the case," Richard continued. "The 9/11 stuff is the smoking gun. The diabolical means these guys are willing to use to..."

"What makes you think the White House was involved?" Hippie asked.

"All we can definitively say at this point..."

"And this is clearly not speculation," Teresa emphasized.

"... is that the official story..."

"At every level, in every aspect..."

"... the official story makes no sense."

"It doesn't explain the most basic facts."

"Like?"

"Oh, like where was NORAD in the most heavily guarded and defended air corridor in the world? Where was the wreckage of the Pentagon plane? Why was there only a tiny hole initially? How could poorly trained pilots pull off such a complex maneuver? Why did the towers explode... "

"Why did steel-constructed buildings fall at all — when they had never done so in the history of architecture?" Teresa added. "And speaking of which, why did Building 7 go down at 5 in the afternoon — poof, in 10 seconds, right over its footprint — when it was never hit by a plane, or by debris, when it never had significant fires — poof?"

"That's the most glaring instance."

"Of?" Hippie asked.

"Of something fishy going on."

"I see."

"We're not saying definitively that the White House did it," T.L. pointed out. "And we can't detail just how things were done... "

"But we know the official story can't be true."

"And we want the public to know that. That alone should... "

"The facts, the unassailable facts — the photos, the videos, the timing of events, the architectural and engineering data, the goddam melting point of steel (Richard was getting worked up) none of this stuff can be explained without assuming some level of government involvement beyond the official story."

"That may be true," Mr. Hippie said, nodding slowly and lidding his eyes. "But people will never believe it."

"We're not asking them to believe it." Teresa said. "We only want them to take in the contradictions, the motives, the alternative explanations."

"There's a book called *The New Pearl Harbor*... "

"I've read it."

"Why didn't you say so? So what do you think?"

"The most important section for your uses is Griffin's list of possible levels of complicity."

"Right! Right!" Richard asserted. "My thought exactly! One through eight. The lowest — just taking advantage of a fortuitous event to effect pre-existing plans... "

"Most people will buy that," Teresa said.

"All the way through level eight, active planning and execution," Richard continued.

"If we could do something to get Americans — hell, just Kansans even — to start thinking in those eight categories... "

"You'd blow open their minds?"

"Right!"

"Right!"

The hosts were firm and united.

Mr. Hippie lidded his eyes again.

"Possible."

"And we have the feeling you may be able to help us... "

He looked fixedly at them.

"Why?"

"Do you want to talk about it?," Richard asked.

Mr. Hippie stood up, and placed his full glass of OJ on the coffee table.

"If I do, I don't right now. It's almost midnight, barbarian time. I need my beauty sleep. It's been nice talking with you. We'll no doubt meet again. Good night."

He walked to the door, followed by his hosts, then turned to them.

"By the way, do you know General Russell?" he asked.

"No," Richard said.

"I see."

"But think about a teaching moment."

Mr. Hippie nodded, and walked out the door. The clock at St. Joseph's struck midnight.

When Gronsky & Skulk had plopped back down on couch and chair, they sat for a moment in silence.

"Well," Richard said, "he's got to be at least <u>interested</u> if he's read Griffin and Frank."

"Yeah, but where is he coming from? He makes me uncomfortable."

"You have too many social skills. Some people don't."

"Still. Creepy is creepy. And he seems just as wary of us."

"He needs to figure whether he wants to get involved."

"And you know what else I think?" Skulk added. "I think he's Skull & Bones."

"You mean... ?"

"Yes. Bush and Kerry Skull & Bones. Secret society. Specializes in weirdness."

"Those guys are all lawyers and government types. Why would someone in Skull... "

"They're also secretive. Doing secret things under cover. What's going on out here that a bonesman might be interested in?"

"I don't know. Not much. Lots of ICBM sites, Cold-war era missile silos... things like... "

"Not much? That's not much?"

"Well they're mostly empty... "

"Mostly? And what about what isn't empty? And what's in there that's not missiles? Government drug operations? I heard about this stuff when I was small enough to sit under the dining room table. I bet he's CIA. Half the agency is bonesmen."

"Don't be ridiculous. He's a department store Santa... "

"Right. Did you notice his ring?"

"No."

"Yale. I used to wear one just like it around my neck."

"So? A lot of strange people go to Yale. You went to Yale."

"And do you know who General Russell is?"

"Who's that? Why?"

"What was the last thing he asked us as he went out the door?"

"I don't remember. A teaching moment."

"No. He asked us if we knew General Russell."

"Who's General Russell?"

"General Russell was the founder of Skull and Bones. 'Do you know General Russell?' is the bonesman formula for identifying other bonesmen."

"You think he thought we were bonesmen? There <u>aren't</u> even any lady bonesmen."

"Oh yes there are. They started recruiting junior women in my senior year — I was past eligible."

"You would have wanted to be?"

"Of course. Starry-eyed, snappy, right-wing blond like me?"

"So that's how you know all this stuff."

"My boyfriend."

"<u>He</u> was... ?"

"Top of the bloodline."

"Who was he... is he?"

"Can't tell you."

"Why not?"

"Secret society. And, damn! I just realized. Do you remember the numbers of the apartment house court he lives in?"

"No."

"318 - 324 Oliver."

"So?"

"Another special bonesman symbol — code, whatever — is the number 322. I bet his address is 322. Now we might know where he lives. We can go look at the mailboxes."

"What makes you think he gave us his real name? Or that the name on the mailbox is his real name? And what's with 322?"

"It's a long story you don't want to hear. Some Greek orator died in 322 BC... "

"Demosthenes died in 322."

"OK, Demosthenes. So the goddess of eloquence... "

"Eulogia."

"Right. Good for the history professor. So Eulogia went away weeping and didn't return until the 19th century when she decided to live in the Tomb — Skull & Bones' clubhouse there on High Street in New Haven. Don't ask me why she chose New Haven. They worship her, the bonesmen. They sing anthems to her. They steal things to offer her — gifts to the goddess. They call themselves the Knights of Eulogia."

"So that's where 322 comes in. Demosthenes."

"And did you notice Hippie's interpolation into the Creation text?"

"No."

"You don't notice much, do you?"

"I notice a lot."

"'And darkness was upon face of the deep.' What comes next?"

"And God said, 'Let there be light.'"

"But what did Hippie say?"

Richard tried to remember.

"Bzzzz. Time's up."

"So what did he say?"

"He said 'Like a tomb.'"

SIXTEEN

Native American

We are calling you, oo-oo-oo, oo-oo-ooo...

So sang the tape loop. The "Indian Love Song". Words no longer by Oscar Hammerstein.

Women's Wear to view, oo-oo-oo, oo-oo-ooo...

Eschewing the mere red, white & blue of other establishments, Kaufmanns had chosen to out-PC the politically correct by honoring pre-colonial, deeper-level denizens: July was Pow-Wow Month at Kaufmann's, celebrating the Keeper of the Plains — that 44 foot high, 5-ton steel sculpture, iconic of Wichita, its face raised toward the sky, its arms lifted in supplication to the Great Spirit — and the Kiowa, Kaw and Kansa tribes that inspired it.

Then you will know
That your love will come true
Kaufmann's styles distill
The essen-tial you...

Since he had not been in touch, Gronsky & Skulk felt they had better check in with Miles Hippie to see what had ensued from their meeting. And there he was, up on his throne with a child on his lap, in front of a teepee (non-Kansan), beside a campfire (simulated by an ingenious stage device involving fans, lights, and flapping silk flames), stained reddish-brown, with arms, legs and torso painted with elemental designs in red, blue and yellow.

"We'll catch him on his break," they thought, and made their way closer to the stage in order to catch his eye. He seemed not to notice.

At their right stood a tobacco-colored man with his six-yearish daughter, all gussied up in a Cinderella princess-dress.

"Indians," Teresa thought, "genuine Kansas Indians!" And she whipped out her recorder for an interview.

"Excuse me, sir," she said politely, "are you Native American?"

"Ugh," he responded.

"What?"

"Uffda! Of course I'm Native American. Do I look Korean?"

"What's 'Uffda'?"

"It means 'oi vey' in Norwegian. I'm sixteenth-blood Kansa, and the rest scandinavian no-goods and mongrel. Jennifer here is thirty-second blood. Say hello, Jennifer."

"Hello."

All shook hands.

"Powerful Kansa genes, in that case," Teresa remarked. "You and Jennifer."

"Mendelian dominant. Culturally subordinate. Politically decrepit."

Teresa hoped she had charged the batteries. This would be a good one.

"Would you mind if I interviewed you on tape? This is Richard Gronsky, my writing partner. He's a history professor at WSU. And I'm Teresa Skulkington. We're doing a book on Kansan opinion about the current political climate, and... "

"Sure. Do I get paid as a contributor?"

"It wouldn't be ethical to pay people for giving opinions. Like in court — You don't get paid for testimony."

"Like hell you don't. What about expert witnesses?"

"Well... "

"I'm an expert witness."

"On?" Richard asked, growing more and more interested.

"On what do you think?"

"Well, at this point, we have no money... ," Teresa responded, hoping to get the discussion on to more practical ground.

"Good. That makes us equal. Neither do I. Always good to deal with equals."

Everyone seemed satisfied except Jennifer, who was anxious to get up to tell Indian Santa what she wanted for her birthday next week. The Cinderella dress was her last year's present and, sizewise, looked it. She pulled the group, via her father's hand, up a line-space as it advanced.

"OK, first question then. What do you, as a Native American, think of all this?" She indicated the stage scenery, props and costumes, and pointed with a wince at the lovelorn loudspeaker. "I mean, it's pretty stereotyping, wouldn't you say — not very PC."

And indeed, Kaufmann's in July was a cornucopia of political incorrectness. Pow-wow month contained a ethics-boggling array of demeaning displays — costume contests, drumming contests (including the white "Indian drummers" of Hamilton JHS), dancing contests to "pow-wow music", an Indian Princess beauty parade, and a warrior walk. Throughout the store were dozens of arts & crafts booths, of both native artists (15% to the store) and anglo school children learning about "Kansas' Indian heritage", while the sixth floor snack bar boasted a July Indian menu featuring buffalo chile with beans and ground buffalo tacos, prepared by Mariott sous-chefs.

"So why do you come here?" Teresa asked.

"Fifty percent off today on selected items for Native Americans."

"Did you get anything?"

The tobacco-colored man drew a Coleman cook stove out of a Kaufmann's plastic bag, and showed it off as if it were an art object or the beginning of a magic trick.

"I didn't realize camping goods were on sale," Teresa said. "I thought that was a winter time thing."

"They're not on sale. Or they are — today. But just for me, not for you."

"How did you know that?"

"The feather."

He pointed to a small plume of down clinging to the side of the stove, like jetsam from some old sleeping bag.

"Didn't you see the sign coming in?"

"I must have missed it," Teresa replied.

"You need an Indian eye. If you're Native American, and you find an item with a feather attached — 50% off. With a driver's license. This is a great stove."

"Don't you feel exploited?"

"Hey, look. $19.99 for an ultra-light butane backpacking stove? $39.99 regular? Who's the exploiter for a change?"

Teresa probed: "You feel your tribe was exploited? How's that?"

"Are you kidding? Don't get me started. We Kansa were supposed to be 'the stupid Indians', the ones who wouldn't — couldn't — give up traditional ways and become Jefferson's 'Christian farmers'. What a load of crap — excuse me, M'am. The whites made sure we couldn't farm. Traders wanted us out hunting to supply their furs, squatters wanted our land, missionaries wanted our souls, and the bureaucrats wanted the money from the sale of the land. Custer's troops were benign in comparison. And what was left for us? Blame. And for you anglos? Absolution from complicity in genocide. Treaties ignored, starvation, a lot of whisky — that's what <u>we</u> got. I'd call that exploitation, wouldn't you?"

"Weren't there many idealists, abolitionists, among the settlers?"

"Yeah, sure. One percent? Two? Even John Brown wasn't so enthusiastic when the skins at risk were red, not black. Most settlers came out for self-serving, economic motives. They were genocidal, environmental exploiters, financed and encouraged by a greedy, moronic, barbarous government."

"I'd agree, Terry," Richard interposed.

"Most historians do," the Indian noted. "Right, Jen?"

His daughter demurred.

"But things have improved now, wouldn't you say? I mean here you are in Kaufmann's — being celebrated. It's PC to love Indians, no?"

"People still want our commodities, not our way of seeing the world. Turquoise jewelry, without the world view. Look at the land. Looted — like us."

"OK. So what do you think of the political situation in general? Now?" Teresa fell back to her standard, effectual, open-ended question. The tobacco-colored man began nodding his head, and pursing his lips. Little Jennifer broke away, and dashed up the steps onto the stage: a stage squaw had cried, "Next!" The trio watched her take her place in the approach-line.

"Before we really start — I forgot to ask — " T.L. said, "what's your name? Say it clearly into the mike — right here, into this little hole."

"Joe Ahlegawaho"

"Can you spell it?"

"Of course. Been spelling it since I was five. A, H, L, E, G, A, W, A, H, O."

"Interesting. What kind of name is that?"

"Full Kansan."

"You said you were only sixteenth-blood."

"Full Kansan identity."

"Like your looks."

"Yeah. Like my looks."

"You're from?"

"Wichita."

"What do you do for a living?"

"I'm an anthropologist. I study Anglo interviewers of Native Americans."

"Get away."

"No, it's true. I study how cultures study one another professionally."

"Fascinating."

"Check out my book, *The Clouded Mirror.* KSU Press."

"We definitely will," Richard said.

"OK then, back to 'what do you think of today's general political situation?'"

"I'll tell you," Joe said. Then, *sotto voce*, but loud enough to attract some stares:

There's a mean black snake
been suckin' my rider's tongue...

There's a mean black snake
been suckin' my rider's tongue,
An if I catch him there, mmmm,
he won't come back no more.
And he crawl up to my window
and he crawl up in my bed
He crawl up to my window
and he crawl up in my baby's bed...
He's a mean mean black snake
that's been suckin' my rider's tongue

"Very nice," Teresa cooed. "I love blues... "

"John Lee Hooker don't just sing the blues, man, he is the blues."

"So what do you think is the mean black snake?"

"You want me to say some person? George? Dick? Condi? It's not people, Ms. Interviewer, it's... "

He paused.

"The system?" Teresa hinted.

"Don't put words in my mouth — interviewing 101."

"Sorry. So what is it?"

"The system — obviously. What else?"

Jennifer was now seated on Mr. Indian Hippie's lap.

"Do you have any thoughts about 9/11?"

"Actually I do. I was on the elliptical at the gym at school... "

"You teach?" Richard asked. "Where?"

"Friends College"

"Ah. Very good."

"... and the TV switches to the towers, one of them smoking. And the first thing I thought of — even before the second plane hit — I thought of this story Bestemor — Grandma — Arneberg used to tell us."

He bit his lower lip and began nodding again, reliving the experience.

"And that was?" T.L. prompted.

"Well, once upon a time there was a clever boy named Per — do you really want to hear this?"

"Of course."

"Of course," Richard echoed. "This is while you were watching the towers go down?"

"... a clever boy named Per, who was gathering nuts along the road, and found a beauty — but with a worm-hole in it. He thought he'd take it home and see if he could find the worm, what it looked like, so he put it in his pocket. On the way, he met the *dejvel*."

"The devil?"

"Sure. Old Nick. Why not? And Per says, 'Is it true you can make yourself as tiny as you want, and even go through the eye of a needle?' 'Of course,' says the devil. 'I can do anything, go anywhere.' Which, of course, he can. 'Could you even creep into... ' — he pulls the chestnut out of his pocket — 'this nut? Right through this tiny hole?' Per says. 'Nothing easier,' said the devil. And whoosh, he did it. A little voice from inside said 'See?'

"'Neat trick,' Per says, and clamps his toothpick right into the hole. Damn if he hadn't captured the devil. Bestemor didn't say damn. Now what to do with him? So he brings the nut to his friend, Henrik the Smith, and he says 'I've got the devil trapped in this nut. What shall we do with him?' 'Let's smash him to bits,' says Henrik, with his hammer was already in hand.' 'OK,' Per says. Smashing — he likes that. They both like that. So Henrik the Smith lays the nut on the anvil, gives it a good whack — but it doesn't break. He hits it harder — still nothing. Bigger hammer, bigger blow. Still nothing. 'Wow,' says the smith, I never saw anything like that.' The original goal of killing the *dejvel* entirely forgotten, this had become a contest of mighty Henrik vs. the physical world. So he grabs the biggest sledge hammer from the wall and gives the nut a blow that would kill an elephant. The nut shatters in a thousand pieces, and he, and Per, and the worm, and the whole smithy are destroyed in the explosion. Only the sledge hammer was left."

"This is what you think about 9/11?" T.L. asked.

Joe nodded.

"And probably the how do you say it *dujvil*, was left, too?" Richard inquired.

Jennifer came skipping back down from the stage, Mr. Hippie watching intermittently, but with attention.

"Hi, kiddo," her dad said. "Did you tell Santa what you wanted for your birthday?"

"Yes."

"What did he say?"

"He told me this weird Indian poem."

"Oh yeah? What was that?"

"And he told me to share it."

"OK, you're sharing it. What was it? Do you remember?"

"*Spirit in the sky,*
Get down here right away
To bite evil's eyes out of his face
So he can't see us."

"Was that it exactly?" Richard asked. "How did you remember all that?"

"He made me say it back to him," the princess replied.

"She has a good memory," her father added.

SEVENTEEN

Dog Days

Inscrutable, he was, Miles Chippie, as he sat once again on their couch. Inscrutable, as in not to be scrutinized, no matter how long one dared to look. Inscrutable, from *scrutari*, "to search – as through trash, *scruta*, "trash or rags."

But <u>was</u> he some kind of trash, Martin Hoppe, was there a soupçon of evil bouquet behind the pricey cologne? The changes were charming, hilarious, well-done – and they were also a tad suspicious, unsettling, <u>too</u> well-done. If not trash, was Michael Happy something other than he seemed, some unknown quantity hiding behind a monosyllabic cloak?

He seemed cool even at 96 degrees, 90% humidity, sitting there in his tropical suit and tie, while Richard was sweating in his sport shirt, and Teresa was taking refuge in her denim cutoffs, which signaled blue across a bare midriff to her white spandex t-shirt above. Her navel made eye at her guest.

"Can I get you something cool?" she asked.

"No, I'm fine, Ma'm, thank you," said Montague Holly.

"Richard and I are having iced tea. It's all prepared..."

"That's all right. I'm good."

"Turn on the air-conditioning?"

"I'm used to the heat."

"You know," Richard noted, "the Romans called these hottest days of summer *caniculares dies*..."

"The Dog Days," Miles noted. "*Hundestage*."

"Why is that?" Teresa asked.

"Their theory," said her beau, "was that Sirius the Dog-Star, the brightest in the sky, in rising with the sun, added to its heat. During the Dog Days, we had to suffer the combined heat of both. But what do we care," Richard noted, "as long as the air-conditioning is working? New diseases? They're for them. Conservation?..."

"Conservation may be a sign of personal virtue, but it's not a sufficient basis for a sound, comprehensive energy policy," Miles said.

"You believe that?" Teresa asked.

"Just quoting Mr. Cheney."

"Oh."

There was an awkward pause.

"Every dogma has its dominion," Miles, non-commital.

"I guess," Richard commented. They're predicting a three to nine degree rise worldwide…"

"Fahrenheit," Miles added.

"Yes. Three to nine degrees by the end of the century if no adequate steps are taken to curb greenhouse gases."

"Mm," commented Miles.

More silence.

"Mr. Hippie, is it me that's making you uncomfortable? I mean I can change into more presentable clothing if…"

"I'm not uncomfortable."

"I mean if…"

"The ardor aroused in men by the beauty of woman can be satisfied only by God."

She didn't know whether to feel complimented or insulted. And again, who was this guy?

"Sexy attire is, of course, subjective," he added, clarifying not at all, though tipping the scale towards insult.

Richard tried to steer the discussion, such as it was, back on track.

"We don't seem to know about all these climate things; we deny it if we do. We don't care, we don't imagine…"

"While that may be true," Miles said coolly, "defaults of consciousness can be remedied. But there's nothing to counter the speeding up of everything. We're in the midst of a full-blown, planet-wide schizophrenia. We make ecological gestures and at the same time proliferate our enterprises of destruction, the performance principle unleashed."

He stood up, and began to pace. Gronsky & Skulk watched him with astonishment.

"Things are irretrievably out of balance, centrifugal, eccentric, driven by inertia. And we have no protection against the perverse effects of our attempts at control. In the name of security, we institute endemic terror in every way as dangerous as the epidemic threat of catastrophe. We force every negative sentiment into clandestine existence. The merest gibe meets with incomprehension. It will soon be impossible to express reservation about anything at all. And this hyper-positivity creates catastrophe.

Can all the 'goodness' be stopped? In a world so full of positive feelings, sentimentality, and self-righteousness? But anything promoting separate notions of good and evil signs its own death warrant. Reality is not naive enough to fall into such a trap."

He sat down once more and stared at his interlaced fingers.

Teresa offered, "We don't seem destined to…"

He glanced up.

"We know <u>nothing</u> about our destination."

C'est tout. It is finished. What more could he say? The three sat silent, imprisoned in impossibility.

"I have been thinking about your proposition concerning a teaching moment — some transcendent act for the country to meditate on — and I've decided to help you."

"Really?" Richard enthused, while Teresa warily looked on.

"We should entertain no illusions about the effectiveness of any kind of rational intervention. We can assume only a slight sensibility valid within the marginal area contributed by thought. Within these bounds, ethical reflection and practical intentions are feasible; beyond them, at the level of process we will have set in motion, there reigns the inseparability of good and evil, and hence the impossibility of evoking one without the other. I say this to spare you the trouble of objecting to my proposition for a transcendent teaching moment."

"Like what?" Richard asked.

"You are right, I think, to point to 9/11 as the key to revolutionary change. You are correct to point to the improbable building collapses as being the parts of the story most vulnerable to exposure. They may have tried to cover their tracks, carting away the steel so quickly, and rebuilding Building 7. But I think you might refresh the screen with a mytho-historical reenactment."

"How is that?" Teresa asked.

"You are going to crash a tiny plane into the Kaufmann building, and bring it inexplicably down. Then you are going to explain it."

"Wait a minute...Now hold on..." they interjected.

"Hear me out."

He said it so peremptorily they had no choice.

"Things are dreadfully confused right now," Miles went on. "What is needed is some daring gesture much like your secession call, profoundly innovative, yet historically resonant and generally admirable. We need to present the public with something it already knows — unconsciously — some extraordinary rendition of the major event of that day. Our task is not so much to answer questions as to raise them, questions that will shed light and <u>heat</u>, and will embarrass the emptiness in people's hearts and minds.

"For that purpose, there is nothing more potent than the historical quotation. The theft of images is an enterprise well rehearsed by capitalism. We are <u>all</u> always engaged in looting the past. You, in addition, will contribute a singular theft from the futurem, an act in collage with the memory-swarm in the collective unconscious, to wit: plane crashes into building, building collapses at freefall speed, directly over its footprint. In the original, the official explanatory sequence was believed. But in ours, never. It will be too ludicrous. And thus will government chicanery be exposed in the light of the contradiction, and it, like the building, will fall. The government."

"But even if we could do it," Richard objected, "people will think it is ridiculous — ludicrous, you said. We'll just be seen as evil clowns..."

"We <u>want</u> the event to be funny. Humor is the cure for their psychotic, crackbrained, consensual hypocrisy."

"So what, exactly, are you proposing we do?" T.L. asked.

"I want you to fly a small Cessna…"

"We don't have a Cessna," objected Richard.

"And we can't fly," added T.L..

"We will steal a Cessna. That's <u>why</u> the Cessna plant is here in Wichita. And you will learn to fly. And you will crash the plane into the top floor of the Kaufmann building…"

"But we'll get killed."

"And we'll kill other pe… "

"Hear me out. You will crash the plane at dawn on Christmas morning, when nobody is in the building or on the streets, and even Santa is heading out of town. No one will get hurt."

"Except us."

"Including you. Since you will have parachuted before contact…"

"We don't know how."

"You will take skydiving lessons. And when you land, you will hold a press conference explaining what the public will have witnessed."

"When they've all been dreaming of sugarplums…"

"The collapse will be caught on video. The press will have been notified. There'll be a special edition of the Wichita Eagle. The New York Times will follow."

This time the silence was charged.

"In the interest of full disclosure," Miles remarked, "I have to say that I consider the press conference a compromise. Our effort is to reach a realm of meaning that is beyond words, but meaningful nonetheless. Compared to the image, words will be paltry, slithering around in the skulls of the masses with unpredictable effect. But the image of the plane half stuck in the building, the image of the building collapsing — <u>that</u> is what will break through the cocoon of habit in which they sleep."

The ice tea was lukewarm now, too soon to be explained by thermodynamics alone.

"How will we bring the building down?"

"I have the tools."

"What tools? Where did you get them?"

"I could tell you, but then I'd have to kill you."

He looked up at two startled faces.

"No, only joking," he assured them. "Leave that to me."

"Won't Kaufmann be ruined?" Teresa wanted to know.

"He wants to rebuild with the insurance money."

"How do you know?"

"Santa knows who's been bad or good."

"What will happen afterwards?" Richard wondered.

"This is a drama with no predictable denouement."

Morton Hopping got up to leave, looking as fresh as when he came. His hosts, on the other hand...

"What about your job?" inquired Teresa.

"I have others," Mark Halprin said.

It would have been gauche to ask what they were.

"Think about it," Malcolm Hopi continued. "Just remember — the absence of a plan is also a plan. And you can call me Miles."

Miles Happie walked out the door, dragging no tail behind him.

EIGHTEEN

Modest Doubt Is Call'd The Beacon of the Wise

Could they do this? Did they even approve of it being done? Violence? Large-scale, possibly lethal violence?

Teresa had never even hunted or fished with Daddy: the idea of threading a worm on a hook had always seemed too yucky. Richard had the comical habit of crushing plastic milk containers with his hands: stomping on them seemed to him unseemly. Now they were challenged to embrace something like... the Truth. Teresa heard Thomas Aquinas urging her from potency to act. Richard felt ripeness was all, and things were very close to ripe.

But both were now smitten by a sudden cloud of fear and abdication. And it was in this eddying mist that they now accompanied WSU's speaker, Rashid Khalidi, towards Levitt Arena on an otherwise cloudless early evening for his talk on "The New American Empire".

Why book the Shockers' home basketball court? Because Khalidi was tall in stature in the academic world? No. Because he was a shocker himself? No. Because this was the summer session's culminating major-speaker event? No. It was because Buildings and Grounds had for some reason denied Richard's request for Wilner Auditorium, though its schedule seemed open. No matter, Richard thought, Levitt will be fine, if slightly less comfortable in the bleachers and folding chairs. Desmond Tutu had spoken there last year, and Khalidi would make a nice followup.

But meteorological cloudlessness was a poor predictor of the gathering storm: streaming up Hillside along with Rashid, Teresa and Richard, were tens, then hundreds of sign-carrying students and community folks. Some wore yarmulkes, most wore crosses, and a scant few sported kuffiyehs, the traditional Palestinian headscarf. Uh-oh, T&R thought, looks like a religious war. Khalid was unruffled. "My fans," he reassured them. *Au courant,* though. The yarmulkas and crosses seemed to populate the same side of the path, while the kuffiyehs and assorted peaceniks lined up sparsely on the other. Law enforcement was nowhere in sight.

ISRAEL BASHERS NOT WELCOME!; TERRORISTS OFF CAMPUS!; EXTREMISTS OUT OF WICHITA!; STUDENTS WILL NOT BE INTIMIDATED!; A NAZI SPEAKER ON TISHA B'AV — SHAME! SHAME!; NEVER AGAIN!; STUDENTS FOR ACADEMIC FREEDOM!; CHRIST SHALL OVERCOME! read signs on one side of the walk.

DIVESTMENT FROM ISRAEL! TROOPS HOME NOW!; WAR IS TERRORISM!; GO SOLAR, NOT BALLISTIC!; ASSES OF EVIL (with pictures of the principals)!; ENFORCE U.N. RESOLUTIONS IN PALESTINE!' ANYTHING WAR CAN DO, PEACE CAN DO BETTER! read signs on the other.

Both sides seemed to share a strong commitment to the exclamation point.

The three of them ran the gauntlet.

The Levitt basketball court had a small stage constructed at one end, as for other large events like rained-out graduations, and Richard and Khalidi took their seats on the well-flowered platform. At 7:40, having allowed ten minutes to accommodate the late-arriving crowd, Richard stood to open the evening.

"Ladies and Gentlemen, Students and Faculty, Members of the Community," he began, "it gives me great pleasure to introduce the final speaker of our Contemporary Issues series, a man who himself has become a contemporary issue. Rashid Khalidi is Edward Said...

Some cheers and boos from the audience. Richard admonished it gently with his famous Groucho waggling-of-eyebrows.

"... Edward Said Professor of Modern Arab Studies and Literature at Columbia University. Professor Khalidi has written more than seventy-five articles on aspects of Middle East history and politics including pieces in the *New York Times* [some boos], the *Boston Globe* [a different set of boos], the *Los Angeles Times*, the *Chicago Tribune*, and many journals. He has received fellowships and grants from the John D. and Catherine T. MacArthur Foundation, the Ford Foundation, and the Rockefeller Foundation, and is a recipient of a Fulbright research award. He has been a regular guest on radio and TV shows, including All Things Considered [applause from the liberals], Talk of the Nation, the NewsHour with Jim Lehrer, and Nightline.

"His latest book, *Resurrecting Empire: Western Footprints and America's Perilous Path in the Middle East*, examines the record of Western involvement in the region and analyzes the likely outcome of our most recent Middle East incursions.

"Let's give a warm welcome to our guest, and I'm sure that, in spite of the controversial nature of his topic, we will show him the respect and hospitality for which Kansas is so justly famous. Ladies and Gentlemen, Professor Rashid Khalidi."

General applause, with a scattering of boos and cheers. Operation Rescue, The Mid-Continent ADL and WSU Hillel stood up in back with their signs.

Khalidi began with many thank-yous for the honor of the invitation, invited questions and discussion after his talk, and launched passionately into his topic.

"Since September 11th, 2001, we've heard a lot about the 'intelligence failures' that left the United States unprepared for the attacks on the World Trade Center and the Pentagon. But these failures were not simply the result of poor espionage or bureaucratic incompetence. They reflected a deeper failure to understand a region and its historical wounds, a number of which — though not all — were inflicted by the Western powers."

Serious pre-uproar among the audience. Khalidi remained calm, but did respond:

"I hope you will agree that the future of America's relations with the Arab and Muslim world depends a great deal on public education. Yet the very people who are in a position to perform this vital task have instead found themselves under siege from the media, from extremist pressure groups and craven politicians. Our crime? Challenging those formidable authorities on the Arab world, George W. Bush, Ariel Sharon and Ehud Olmert."

Standing and yelling from the audience:

"Anti-semite!"

"If you don't like it here, go home!"

"Nazi Jew-killer!"

"Terrorists off campus!"

Richard stepped forward, and took the mike from the lectern.

"Ladies and Gentlemen, this kind of behavior will have reverberations country-wide. Internationally. This is an institution committed to academic freedom! Please, please, reserve your comments until after Professor Khalidi's talk, and then keep them polite. Believe me, the whole world is watching." He inserted the mike once again in its holder and took his seat. Khalidi, continued, apparently unflustered.

"Back in 1992, a decade before 9/11, a group of right-wing thinkers from the administration of the first George Bush created the Project for a New American Century, PNAC. I strongly suggest you google them, and study their documents closely. Their platform demanded that the United States take advantage of the fall of the Soviet Union to achieve unchallenged, unchallengeable domination of the planet, and control of its dwindling resources. They called on America to substantially increase its military budget, to deny other nations the use of outer space, and to adopt a more aggressive and unilateral foreign policy that would allow it to act offensively and preemptively in the world. The elimination of states like Iraq figured prominently in this grand vision.

(Applause and a quickly abating "U-S-A! U-S-A!")

"In a widely-circulated 1998 letter to President Clinton, the members of PNAC — Donald Rumsfeld, Paul Wolfowitz, Eliot

Abrams, Richard Armitage, Richard Pearl, Robert Zoellick, William Kristol and Francis Fukayama among them — challenged the president to move forcefully and militarily to remove Saddam Hussein.

(Again some applause, with annoyed shushing from the liberals.)

"And in their defining document, "Rebuilding America's Defenses", written in Sept 2000 — a full year before 9/11 — they acknowledged that the process of transformation was likely to be a long one, absent — in their own chilling words — 'some catastrophic and catalyzing event like a new Pearl Harbor.' One year later that event would arrive."

It was time for the Blintz Brigade, a group whose motto was "Cream Pies Are For Cream Puffs!" From left and right, two nightmare gaggles of yarmulka-ed, gabardined clowns invaded the platform, firing blintzes at the speaker, splattering his dark suit with crème fraiche ("For The Blessed, Nothing But The Best!"), and greasing the ground with doughish offal.

Now a blintz is no mere crêpe. The baked and semi-hardened dough raised second-degree welts and third-degree contusions on Professor Khalidi's face — and let loose bedlam in the audience.

Richard sprang from his seat, and Teresa ran up on stage to help battle the clowns. In the arena, folding chairs clattered as the yarmulkas attacked the kuffiyehs, and the crosses attacked them both and one another. Neutrals scattered at first, then tested out testosterone in random directions. Even women have testosterone.

Enter the campus police. Exit the campus police. This was more than they could handle.

The uproar grew from forte to fortissimo as the entropy increased. The clowns had disappeared. Poof! On stage, Richard and Teresa were madly wiping down the distinguished professor with hankie and scarf.

Sirens without, and onto the stage poured the burly Wichita police in an overly-tactical rear-entrance maneuver. With macho seriously compromised from slipping all over the spent blintz shells, they nevertheless succeeded in throwing an orange net over Teresa, Richard and Khalidi before confronting the audience. This latter they did from the edge of the platform, using academy sharpshooters to practice with the new paint-ball and itch-powder 12-gauge shotguns. The chaos on the court was enhanced by scratching and sneezing and wiping of semi-enameled eyes.

Paint transmuted into war-paint, during which the orange-net enforcers, donning ski-masks, resorted to the old-style tactics of punching, kneeing and kicking their capturees. "This is what you get when you fuck with us!" one blue-garbed protector informed Teresa.

Yet more sirens, and more again. The Kansas State Police had not had a chance to try out the $15.3 million worth of advanced tactical weapons they had amassed from the Homeland Security Gift Shop and Café. The gym-space echoed anew with concussion grenades; rubber bullets bounced off walls and public; bean-bags (aka FBs, or "flexible batons") crescendoed the havoc while wooden dowels percussed from skulls to floor.

Was there reaction? You bet!

Anarchists in the crowd organized an ad-hoc protest by stripping naked and arranging themselves non-hierarchically in a peace sign, and were soon trampled by old hippies in tie-dyes and ponytails shouting ancient slogans, and threatening to call the ACLU.

This was too much for the mid-level officers, who up till now had let the rookies rock and roll. Out came the temporarily-blinding strobe lights, and then the Tasers which, in case you haven't been following, fire barbed darts which deliver a 50,000 volt jolt. Those hit lose muscle control (including sphincters), and collapse instantly. The gym floor became littered with bodies, clothed and un-, and their offal.

Still there was resistance from the quickly-erected holding pens. Insufferable: chanting and most provocative of all, video-taping and flashbulbs. It was time for DARPA-level crowd control using weapons that had never been used, not in Wichita, not in

Kansas, not in the continental United States, save possibly at the U1a Facility at the DOE's Nevada Test Site — and maybe not even there. Semi-conductor lasers to create plasma "flash-bangs" stunning and disorienting the target; heat-compliance weapons — directed-energy prototypes that would instantly raise body-temperature to an intolerable level. Taser-type darts variously tipped with four varieties of incapacitating, psycho-active drugs.

But alas, before any of these could be brought into play, the gym lights went out. The clowns had struck again. Several hands copped major feels on Teresa. This was not to her liking. Richard's hammerlock was tightened through the net, and Khalidi was only just recovering from the baton-twirling routine especially for Ragheads. Then the sprinklers came on strong, dampening the mood and the firepower. And a Jewish clown laugh-track filled the room, with arena loudspeakers cranked up to max — which is pretty loud.

Then silence. Blackness and wetness and silence. The evening seemed over. The police withdrew, fading out under cover of darkness, walkie-talkies crackling obscurely, diminuendo to nothing. The audience walked, limped, staggered, crawled, swam to freedom.

The next day, the *Wichita Eagle* quoted Mayor Mayans as declaring the police action "a model for homeland defense," and noted that all officers had demonstrated "an enormous amount of restraint," and were thus able "to refrain from arrests."

Of the three on the platform, one began to entertain modest doubts about remaining in his adopted country, while on a related subject, the other two harbored no more doubts whatsoever.

URGENT

WHEN IN THE COURSE OF HUMAN EVENTS

it becomes necessary for one people to dissolve the political bands which have connected them with another... "

Remember those words from grade school? Remember Tom Jefferson saying we need a revolution every seven years to keep the government straight? Well, it's been almost 150 years since statehood, and we still haven't gotten it together. Against?

Against losing our sons and daughters in an illegal, must-lose war. Against losing our jobs to sweatshops overseas, and our unions to corporate control. Against the lies, secrecy and corruption of the federal government, with its increasing power-grab, threatening our states' rights. Against the destruction of our beloved Kansas land, and the forced decay of our towns and cities. Against federally mandated welfare for the rich. Against the sacrifice of our domestic needs to feed an overstuffed military.

KANSANS UNITE AND DISUNITE!

It is time to relive our heroic roots as the Free Territory of Kansas! It is time to dissolve our bands to a government, bent on dragging America — and the world — to destruction. Our Kansas Constitution allows us to secede. The U.S. Constitution does not forbid it.

A spectre is haunting the suffering world. But the prairie fire is lit. Join with other Kansans to demand a bill declaring secession, and the resurrection of a territory dedicated once more to freedom! And thus begin the most exciting time of your life. For more information, contact freekansas@yahoo.com, or visit our website at www.freekansas.org.

rgronsky@wsu.edu
www.freekansasagain.org

TWENTY

Conspiracy Theory

Birds conspire, bees conspire. Even educated fleas conspire. Everything that lives con-spires, breathes together — including the hermit in his mountain cave, whose chromosomes are in league with the rest of humanity. And much of this universal conspiring goes on behind the closed doors of language, of geography, of universe of discourse. Do we really know what the termites discuss?

But all someone has to do is say the words "conspiracy theory", and all listening, all speculation — all thinking — closes down. "Conspiracy theory? I'm not going there!" All commentary becomes derisive, all investigation is disparaged, facts are sidelined, evidence dismissed: "Conspiracy theory". The term floats over the world like cloudlets of cling-wrap, ready to seal up thought at the least shiver of fear, or the first threat to power. In the cognitive witch hunt, ideas take cover. The Revenge of Dow Chemical, with Saran-Wrap as Torquemada.

But this state of affairs obtains in merely the great world outside. In the little world of 632 Second St. Apt 4K, Wichita, "conspiracy theory" had all the trappings of praxis — the free, creative and self-creative activity through which humans create and change their historical world and themselves.

"First of all," Miles said, "You've got to try to find every copy of that thing you put out yesterday."

"What's wrong with it?"

"What's wrong is that you guys are going to be tracked before the Event. You don't want an audience just yet, thank you."

"But we need to prepare the ground," T.L. said.

"We need to issue a call to the people of Kansas," Richard added. "How else will they know what the Event is all about?"

"The call is fine," Miles advised. "it just can't be traceable to <u>you</u>. Get your email address off the thing. And your personal website. You've got to find every copy you can. How many did you give out?"

"We put out five hundred, in about thirty or forty drop spots."

"Five hundred in each spot?"

"No. Divided among them. You know — convenience stores, ATM places, mom and pop... "

"Plus we put up some on bulletin boards," Richard noted.

"Do you know where you put them all?"

"We made a list."

"OK. Let's divide up the places, and head out right now. Back here when we're finished. You have an apartment key for me?"

"Um... " Teresa hesitated.

"Yes. Sure." Richard offered. "Here. Take mine. I'll get my spare."

"Fine. You take the motorcycle. T.L., you take the car. I'll use my bike. I want us all back here in 45 minutes. Possible?"

"Uh... probably," Richard thought.

1:10 later:

"... and 242 makes... 499," T.L. said.

"Plus mine," Miles added.

"Fuck!" Richard expostulated. "Not one taken. Not one! Except for you."

"Only 16 hours," said Miles. "Can't tell how many read the posted ones though," he observed.

"Right. It may not be a total loss."

"You mean it may not be a total save," Miles corrected. "You don't want that information out there. Now there'll be a little cloud of unknowing around security."

"But how will we get the information out?" Richard asked.

"You need a non-traceable website and email address. And you can do your drops — but not in Wichita. Make them think the perps are elsewhere."

"Like where?" T.L. wanted to know.

"How about John Brown's Osawatomie?"

"Good. Clearly symbolic." Miles opined. 'Osawatomie' could be just a political statement — or a state of mind. And didn't you say you were thinking about a safe house?"

"It came to mind," T.L. affirmed.

"So you can have a safe house for the publication – not in Osawatomie. Print and mail out from there."

"Where's there?"

"Anywhere but here – or Osawatomie. Farther better than closer."

"Who do we mail to? Just our friends? We've got to do drops."

"Mail to anyone. Mail a hundred at random. The feds will pick it up, believe me. You think those scanners look only at addresses on printed matter?"

T.L. brought Miles a glass of OJ, and once again noticed his ring.

"Did I tell you I went to Yale, too?" she asked.

"No," he said.

"Class of '93."

He nodded.

"When were <u>you</u> there?" she asked.

"Long before you," he answered.

So much for alumni talk.

"Are you ready to go over the plan?" Miles asked.

They sat down across from him. T.L. would take notes.

"General objective: to create an Event which will give the lie to the administration's version of 9/11, specifically to the collapse of the towers and Building Seven. The Event will be designed to demonstrate that controlled demolition duplicates, and far better explains the destruction observed on that day. Are we agreed?"

"Yes."

"Yes."

"You are to liberate a small Cessna from the Cessna plant in the early hours of Christmas morning, and fly it into the upper floors of the Kaufmann Building. I will supply the flight training software needed to do this. Correct?"

"Correct."

"Correct. I've always wanted to learn to fly," added Richard.

"At this point, I think it important to revisit the idea of the press conference, which I floated earlier, perhaps too hastily," Miles said.

"If we can learn to parachute…"

"Of course you can learn. But is that the most effective thing to do? For The Kause?"

"What do you mean?" T.L. asked suspiciously.

"We agree, do we not, " Miles asked, "that adopting The Kause will require enormous leaps of imagination and faith from a midwestern population steeped in ignorance and slumbering in the Big Lie?"

Richard and T.L. both nodded.

"And remember that the Big Lie is not merely that of Goebbels and Orwell," Miles added. "Our friends in Washington have taken it to a new, previously unimagined, dimension – lying about this, and then that, and that, and that, so that the lies reach critical mass and metastasize, spread like a cancer eating at the very notion of truth itself. The Lie-All-Pervasive. And brazen. And bald. And better that we <u>know</u> all is lying."

Miles got up, and began to pace.

"Pilate asked 'What is truth?'" he continued "Today we answer – and <u>inductively</u>, for we know it to be the case, 'There is no such thing.' And so why bother investigating?"

"That's why people…" T.L. began.

"That's why people," Miles pushed on, "do not probe. But beyond that, as you have no doubt observed, they embrace their ignorance. They mumble that 'knowledge is power.' But ignorance is far *more* powerful. In a week, ignorance can destroy what knowledge has taken centuries to build up."

"In a day. In an hour," Richard observed. "Look at 9/11."

"Precisely," Miles allowed. "Ignorance destroys records, memory, and loses the skills and the keys. 'Let there *not* be…' ignorance says – and it is so. While knowledge labors under stricture of scruple, ignorance is free, ready to bring down blind the pillars of the temple and revel in its destruction."

He took a long swig of OJ and sat down again. T.L. wrote down his words like the A student she had always been.

"So your task – The Event's task — is huge – far more than a simple demonstration of technical fact. You have to commit a work of art so powerful as to break all Blake's mind-forged manacles."

"Right."

"Right."

They both assented. Yes.

"Do you really think you can do that with anything less than your deaths? Were not the kamikaze pilots, are not the suicide bombers, far more impressive and convincing than the cowards who push buttons from afar, and whine at the least scratch? Don't you *need* to impress and convince by dying?"

A profound silence reigned in Apartment 4K. Miles took another mouthful of OJ.

"If the plane hits, and the building comes down, what's to prevent them from spinning it the same way: old building, weak construction, airplane fuel…?" T.L. wondered.

"I think we have to perform it," Richard said, "– almost like a carney act: drum roll, point, building collapses, 'ta-daaaa!', and then an explanation of how the trick worked, and how exactly it duplicated the collapses of the 9/11 buildings."

"You can never overestimate the stupidity of the public," T.L. noted.

"But at the same time," Miles observed, "you run the equally great, perhaps greater, risk of appearing as just another set of talking heads, or another pair of whackos, waving your Unabomber thesis for the media. Jaded, they are, and destitute of moral imagination. We're all doomed to death, so why not use <u>yours</u> in the most provocative way? You want to be carney hucksters, or change-agents?"

They considered the question, each alone with self.

"You'll have to let us talk this over by ourselves," Richard said. "In the mean time, let's discuss the original plan for a press conference."

T.L. nodded agreement.

Miles lidded his eyes, and nodded his head slowly.

"All right then," he said, "It's your decision. Back, for the moment, to Plan A. You'll enroll today with Suraci Freefall and Skydiving."

"Don't we need to learn to fly first?" Richard asked.

"October is the last month of the season for skydiving lessons. You can learn to fly during November and December in the controlled comfort of this very room — since you seem to prefer comfort to hardship..." Not too subtle, Miles, when being snide. "I'll take care of the rest."

In early October, Richard was interviewed by the FBI for having (out of curiosity) checked the following books out of the WSU Library: Helen Liss, The Loizeaux Family of Controlled Demolition, Inc., *Demolition: The Art of Demolishing, Dismantling, Imploding, Toppling and Razing*, and The Dalai Lama, *Advice on Dying*.

TWENTY-ONE

The Angels of the Lord Will Bear You Up.

The decision wasn't that difficult. He was a teacher, she, a lecturer; press conferences were more natural to them than death. Besides, each had always wanted to sky dive. On the other hand, both were terrified to do it.

Suraci Freefall was <u>the</u> place to go in Wichita. It was also the only place. The "aviation capital of the world" seemed so confident in its many abilities to take off and land, it had almost neglected this occasionally useful training. And Kansans are in general so straight as to make leaping into empty air from five figure altitudes about as likely as a parachuting pig — Suraci's jolly logo. So to Suraci they would go.

Miles spelled out the drill beforehand: they would each start with a tandem jump to overcome their fears — strapped onto the belly of a jump master, free-falling from 12,000 feet, opening the canopy at five, and landing safely with him or her. As many tandem jumps as needed to become comfortable. He would take care of the fees. Next, they would take and graduate from a USPA Static Line Course — six hours of training on all aspects of jumping, focusing on canopy control and safety, and culminating in a solo jump from 3,000 feet, with the parachute opening automatically, the rip-cord attached to the plane, as in the old World War II films. This training was all they would need, since The Event would be accomplished static-line. If they wanted, and time was left in the season, they could proceed to the Accelerated Free Fall Course, just for extra experience, and the thrill of falling. After their certification, Miles himself would train them for the specifics of the task at hand. He seemed to know what he was talking about.

On their drive over to Suraci, Miles reassured them about death. Each year, he reported, about 35 people died skydiving, out of 2 million jumps. Given the odds, he opined, you're better off skydiving than you are, say, shark-cage diving. Every year, about 46,000 people die in traffic accidents, so if you're concerned, he advised, "you can get out of the car right now." They didn't. There was additional information: about 2,500 die motorcycling, and about 80 are killed by lightning. Somehow, they weren't comforted.

The day was warm for late September. Suraci consisted of an acre of grass, two trailers, an open-walled shelter, and a runway out in an ocean of cornfield. Lounging in the shelter, waiting for the sky to clear were about a dozen young people and a few older folks — the trainers. The T-shirts were lively —

DEFINE NORMAL.

WHAT COULD POSSIBLY GO WRONG?

MOST SPORTS NEED ONLY ONE BALL — MINE TAKES BOTH!

— their wearers even livelier, fueled by adrenergic anticipation.

They were directed to the office trailer, where they proceeded to sign their lives away. Seventeen pages of waivers, sign here, initial there, Suraci is in no way responsible for anything (initial), anytime (initial), anywhere (full signature) I will not attempt to sue, no matter what — death, dismemberment, paralysis, broken bones, sprained ankles, even in the case of gross negligence. (How can you sue, after all, if you're dead?) Not a very encouraging introduction. "Just formalities," a peppy young woman behind the counter assured them

WHEN THE PEOPLE LOOK LIKE ANTS-PULL.

WHEN THE ANTS LOOK LIKE PEOPLE-PRAY.

"No danger at all."

The "training" for the tandem jump took fifteen minutes — essentially just a description of what would happen, a suiting-up, and during takeoff, a strapping on, back to instructor belly.

There <u>was</u> an initial crisis: a T.L.-fashion emergency. She couldn't find a suit that fit her. The Ss were too loose, and the XSs too short and tight. She went for the S, and pinned up the excess fabric into the form-fitting style which was her wont. The helmets, too, were too large for her elegant small-headedness, but by reclaiming the bun of her pre-teen ballet days, she managed to get one adequately fixed.

It was the final flight of the day, the sunset flight, with two first freefallers and their divemasters and photographers, and Teresa and Richard strapped in their tandems. The instructors were happy to climb to the Beechcraft's higher altitude. "More time in freefall," thumbs up, a celebration not all in the cabin shared.

At 14,000 feet, the door was opened, and the freefallers executed their routines. As the two sets of three fell away from the plane, they disappeared quickly from sight. Ladies first, in this beer-culture crew. Teresa and Joe, her burly tandem master, took their siamese place at the open door.

The gorgeous Kansas sunset was the most frightening she had ever seen. "I'm not supposed to be doing this," she thought. "Why are my legs dangling two miles above the ground?" Joe's yell through her helmet seemed not to the point: "Ready to jump?" What was she supposed to say at this point, in this place, and Miles having paid 200 bucks? 'No?'. In any case, Joe didn't wait for an answer. He pushed her out in front of him, and together they trod the Newtonian measure, $d = \frac{1}{2} gt^2$. The 120 mph wind screamed past her ears. Joe mimed behind her — head back, hips forward, then arms out, and she caught his body language, and did her best to imitate. "Good going!" he yelled.

It was hard to breathe. The straps were like to bisect her. Was she really falling? The sensation was not what her terrified imagination had expected, but more like floating on a strong wind, not frightening, but awesome — if she didn't think of the splat-like consequences maybe 12,000 feet below. Starlet in the theater of gravity she was, sliding down the sky, dead weight to Joe, but alarmingly alive.

Thirty, forty, fifty seconds of this improbable rapture of the deep, then SWOOSH... JERK — and silence — amazing, contrasting, colossal silence, suspended in space below a rainbow canopy. Turning and turning in the widening gyre, no falcon could be heard, no plane, no truck, no voice within. Only the knowing of wonder.

After a minute or so, a bromidic god-voice behind her, "Having fun?"

He took her silence for a 'yes'.

The landing was gentle and precise. "Congratulations," Joe said. She turned around and kissed him full on the lips.

Richard had a parallel, though gender-bent experience. With Sheila's ample chest pressed against his muscled back, he had felt ready to embrace the siren of falling. His fear was less than his partner's. Perhaps it was the logo on Sheila's T-shirt, displayed before she jump-suited up: ONLY SKYDIVERS KNOW WHY THE BIRDS SING. But what he thought of staring out the door, 14,000 feet down, was nothing more or less than Bob and Ray's old signoff, "It takes a heap of flyin' to make a man a bird." That, and a plan, and 200 bucks, and 3 mg/ml adrenalin, and... "Out we go!"

When the chute opened, and he could actually see, the red sun on the yellow fields was stupefyingly sublime. If Icarus and Lucifer had fallen from an excess of pride, Richard's fall was marked only by humility. Gravity was his dharma, gratefulness his reply. When Sheila called out a river to his right, he looked left. "No. Your <u>other</u> right," she chided. All was right: all was one. He landed and sported a huge grin for the rest of the day and evening. People on the street thought he was in love.

Miles was happy all had gone well, and talked them through the next week's training, the six-hour Static Line Course, and six solo jumps from 3,000 feet with no real freefall, and far less feel-good soaring. The point was to learn to accurately steer their parachutes for landing in compromised, tight conditions, close to water, buildings, and power lines.

By mid-October, global warming had turned the weather cold, precluding further practice. Miles promised he would obtain for them (don't ask) the most advanced special ops-type, state-of-the-art, immediate-deployment systems with optimal steering control. They'd be jumping from no more than 500 feet, as they angled their plane downward towards the 150 foot building, and left it a half mile short of contact for a drop zone in Herman Hill Park. They should start praying now for a wind-free day.

Joining in leaps that might land in the next world was a bonding without compare. As they fell, and watched the other falling, they fell ever more in love. As they gracefully landed, they landed in mutual grace. As they prepared for The Event, beyond hobby, beyond sport, they became a team first and foremost, a cadre of two, a cell, a cabal, a secret society.

They were Richard and T.L. no more, but Gronsky & Skulk forever. Not everybody gets the chance to live like this.

TWENTY-TWO

Prairie Fire 3

20 October, 2006

My Dear Children,

It is hardly meet for me to do so, but I would ask that you consider again the value of sacrifice — even unto death. For how much greater is suffering than any mere explaining!

Remember that the Lord Himself refused to have angels bear him up should he cast Himself down from the pinnacle of the temple. Instead, He chose to experience the full weight of unmerited anguish that He might purchase for us everlasting life, and joy, and glory.

If the very Christ Jesus chose to die for us, what better recompense, what more appropriate response, than to return our blood for His, and with it to wash slavery off the map of this great territory? Such sacrifice may well be needed to awaken people from the deep sleep that has settled upon their minds.

It is stern stuff, to be ready to go where the Master calls, to act as He did, and do as His example bids us. But as we appeal to the Supreme Judge of the world for the rectitude of our intentions, so with His stripes may we be healed. Our deaths may be of vastly more value than our lives.

My children, be not afraid. Whatever calamity beckons, we may feel quite cheer–ful in the assurance that God reigns and will overrule all for His glory and the best possible good. The angels of the Lord <u>will</u> bear us up, and the sufferings of men cannot imprison, chain or hang the soul. I cannot remember a night so dark as to have hindered the coming day, nor a storm so furious or dreadful as to prevent the return of warm sunshine and a cloudless sky.

Yours in faith,

John Brown

TWENTY-THREE

Liberal, Kansas

What better place than Liberal, KS for a safe house for Gronsky & Skulk? So center-left a name as to be plausible, yet so L-word as to be impossible for so radical a mission. Confusing, too, the address. For they had found a tiny house for rent at 632 Second Street, the same numbers as their own in Wichita, a one-roomer clapboard, as perfect a housing for an old, *samizdat* printing press — as a pump house is for a pump. Such a conflation of alphanumerics was bound to be confounding to investigators, a subtle misdirection inducing homeland security doubt. Yet why rent the place at all, why spend the money, when a simple P.O. Box would do? (needs for application form?) And imagine their elation when the box assigned them was #3461 — the date (1861) when Kansas was admitted to the union as a free state, the 34th. Clearly a sign.

Liberal, KS. Population 19,666 at the last census, home of The Land of Oz pocket theme park, the Mid-America Air Museum (fifth largest air museum in the country), and National Helium, Inc., the world's largest helium extraction plant. Perfect. More than perfect: a main east-west drag — Pancake Blvd. — for Liberal is also the home of the International Pancake Race between the housewives of Liberal and Olney, England, held annually on Shrove Tuesday, which heralds the fasting of Lent. Why this was the über-omen for G&S is worthy of our only footnote.[1] So, yes, Liberal, KS 67901 — safer than most.

---

[1] Gronsky & Skulk imagined America as poised on the edge of a grand penitence, about to experience the desert of its own emptiness, and overcome – or not – the temptations with which it was enmeshed. Shrove Tuesday was a time for confessing – as America soon must do — and for cleansing the cupboards of milk, eggs and butter, symbolic of its global obesity.

Pancakes were the perfect medium for consuming the soon-to-be-forbidden. And they both loved pancakes. Back in 1445, in Olney, England, a woman had been cooking pancakes when she heard the church bell calling the faithful, and raced, discombobulated, out of the house and all the way to church

On the afternoon they'd driven out to scout for safety, they'd noticed a flyer on the community bulletin board at the post office:

ALTERNATIVE JIHAD
A Talk by Bernard McGuirk, Ph.D.
Weds, October 25, 7PM
at the Unitarian-Universalist Fellowship
247 Harold Blvd., Liberal.

Sounded interesting enough to warrant a sleepover instead of a long drive back to Wichita that night, a way to check out the political lay of the land. They had hoped to be anonymous, a pair of flies on the church wall. But the Fellowship turned out to be a small storefront in a crumbling shopping mall, and not only were they <u>not</u> anonymous, they were distinguished celebrities, the only new faces to have shown up in the tiny congregation in the last several years, and therefore elaborately greeted and quizzed by the town's embattled eponyms.

They thought it best to use their pre-agreed pseudonyms and stories, version 1. So that night Aaron Fortunato (he, dark) and Heidi Freund (she, blond), visitors from Mill Valley, California, heard Bernie McGuirk expostulate as follows:

"Friends,

"Most of you were present at last month's vigil, and observed for yourselves the results of our first experiment with an open mike. For those not there, and for our honored guests from California, let me say that in the course of half an hour, no one accepted our offer to speak. There <u>were</u> three bystander comments — perhaps 'by-walker' would be more accurate — three comments, each from a young man, approximately eighteen to twenty

---

still holding her frying pan. Embarrassed and awkward, she gave the pancake to the bellringer, and from him received a fabled kiss.

The race to salvation Gronsky & Skulk imagined as theirs to win, and the kiss the seal of their love.

years old, yelled out *en passant*. The first and most clever was 'Make war, not love!' Not, perhaps, original, but showing at least a spark of social satire. The second *cri de coeur*, perhaps fifteen minutes later, was 'You s-dash-dash-k!' He said the word; I will not. And the third observation, just before the end of the vigil, more a mutter than a cry, was 'I thought all the Commies were dead!' It was quite disappointing."

Bernie was a huge man with a great overhanging belly, and a face that seemed to be bursting out of his head. His voice, however, was high and small.

"Louder, please.," was the request.

He did his best to comply by coming around to the front of the lectern, and holding his papers in hand.

"I thought a great deal about this," he continued, "and would like to share my reflections with you here tonight."

Heidi took her tape recorder out of her purse. and checked with her neighbor about using it. "Sure, go for it," he whispered firmly, "We have nothing to hide."

"Americans," Bernie was saying, "<u>most</u> Americans — deplore the violence afflicting contemporary youth, and look toward Hollywood or rap as its prime sources. The president — this well-armed Mr. Malaprop — announced that while we may never know what causes such violence, 'We' — quote — (here he consulted his notes) 'we do know that we must do more to reach out to our at-risk youth and teach them to express their anger and to resolve their conflicts with words, not weapons.'

"I suppose Liberal's three youth-pundits were doing just that, and might even deserve some Presidential Award for not shooting up a dozen commie peaceniks who s-dash-dash-k — with legally concealed weapons. Still, before presenting their award, our leaders might consider that these three young men are being doped — I use the word advisedly — by their own military planners and recruiters, by the national glorification of our national military violence, and by the illegal behavior of the military (I don't want to upset you, and this is my opinion only, but I must call them) the military <u>terrorists</u> under their direction."

The crowd received this blandly enough.

"Those young people were raised on triumphal American brutality. They have seen feel-good presidents bomb Iraq, Sudan, Yugoslavia, and now Afghanistan and Iraq once more — and they too, our youth, feel good about it. Why shouldn't they, since our leaders model their satisfied violence, our media trumpets it, and the population as a whole eats it up — as long as few of them, and none of us — are hurt. Support the troops!

Well, I believe — and I'm not speaking for the group, just my own opinion — that it's time for us to respond more actively to this situation."

Some indecipherable murmuring greeted the potential demand.

"Who is us? We liberals — and I say the L-word proudly — we humanists, U-Us, secularists, agnostics even atheists, we freethinkers — we too need to be heard, deserve to be heard, and not ignored and insulted, considered less worthy than those whose faith is based on mythology, rather than on logic, science, and verifiable history.

"Now I'm not saying that those whose lives are based on myth are any more ignorant than ourselves, or that we, with our advanced degrees, are morally superior. (General agreement). Mythologies have often made humans better and, at times, saved them in ways rationality simply can't — preventing suicides, preserving families, helping some conquer mountains. So if anyone wants to pray to any of the gods, that's fine by me. (Hearty head-nodding.) But that is not the issue."

He paused here to find his lost place among the sheets of paper.

"The issue is... ." (Still hunting the right sheet)... "the issue is, we need to get more aggressive, to have the guts and the conviction to let the conservatives know where we stand — the way those young men shouted out at us. We don't have to be nasty like them. We can do it nicely. We don't have to use bad language. But as people have a right to their extremism, so we have a right to be moderate.

"We need to go on a new kind of jihad — a jihad from our side, the middle side, the nice side, as it were, a jihad of grown-ups with brains enough to understand the difference between politics and faith-based opinion.

"We are everywhere, after all. And we didn't have to be born again, or swear any kind of blood oaths to get there. But we too have to get onto talk shows, and television, and provide a calm, well-reasoned alternative to the nut-case performers out there. We have to show ourselves as moderate, attractive, able to really raise the substantive questions in a non-ideological way. We have to put... nice people into government again."

He was still struggling with the papers.

"Well, I can't find where I was supposed to be, but that's really about all I wanted to say. In short, that that's the kind of jihad we need now — an enlightened counter-jihad to counter the dark — and I'm not talking race here — the dark jihad we are being assaulted with. OK, that's it... Thank you."

He sat down to small, but genuine applause.

"Oh. I forgot to say that sincerity isn't enough. Just because you believe things doesn't make them true. Thank you again."

The discussion that followed was well-intentioned.

As Aaron & Heidi walked back to their B&B, they were more determined than ever on The Event.

Parked outside their porch, was a pickup truck which raised the substantive question *IF GUNS ARE OUTLAWED, HOW CAN WE SHOOT LIBERALS?*

Osawatomie RAG

THE FREE TERRITORY OF KANSAS

The Free Territory of Kansas is a peaceful, democratic, grass-roots solidarity movement committed to the return of Kansas to its rightful status as an independent republic.
Members subscribe to the following principles

1. Political Independence. Our primary objective is to extricate Kansas peacefully from the United States as soon as possible.

2. Direct Democracy. We favor devolution of power back to local communities and the extension of participatory democracy to the workplace and the farm.

3. Sustainability. We celebrate and support Kansas' small, clean, green, sustainable, socially responsible towns, farms, businesses, schools, and churches.. We also believe that energy independence is an essential goal.

4. Economic Solidarity. We encourage Kansans to buy locally produced products from small local merchants rather than from giant, out-of-state mega stores.

5. Quality Education. We would return to local Kansan communities the control and financing of small local schools.

6. Wellness. We encourage locally controlled health care systems in which, unlike the United States, patients, physicians, clinics, hospitals, and insurance providers are all in community.

7. Nonviolence. We do not condone state-sponsored violence inflicted either by military or law enforcement officials. We are unconditionally opposed to any form of military conscription.

8. Foreign Policy. We favor negotiations with similar-minded states and provinces of Canada to create a Free Territory Confederacy with membership in the U.N.

9. Membership. Free Territory of Kansas membership is open to anyone who subscribes to these principles, regardless of race, religion, gender, or sexual orientation.

FOR MORE INFORMATION email us at freekansas@yahoo.com, or visit our website at www.freekansas.org.

COMMUNIQUÉ number 1

TWENTY-FIVE

Frustration

From the standpoint of psychoanalysis, "frustration" refers to the denial of gratification by reality. When, for a mentally healthy person, the environment is not prepared for the acceptance of a libidinal urge, it may be held in suspension until reality is suitably arranged, or until some form of substitute gratification presents itself. Frustration may thus be eluded by sublimation.

When the urge cannot be controlled by the subject, he may summon all his energies to the satisfaction of the urge, disregarding the mores of his surroundings. Or he may regress, and withdraw from reality to take refuge in fantasy-life.

Many works of art spring from such energies.

Sometimes such works of art are visited upon large populations.

Osawatomie RAG

WHAT'S THE MATTER WITH YOU?? WHY DON'T YOU ANSWER US??

Since we have yet to receive any hits or emails, the Osawatomie RAG presents a special 3-page Communiqué listing some of the more obvious questions concerning the events of 9/11.
If thinking about them doesn't make you think about secession, nothing will.

THE WORLD TRADE CENTER COLLAPSES

— What caused World Trade Center Building 7, a 47-story steel skyscraper never struck by any aircraft and with only minimal fires, to collapse at 5:20 p.m. on 9/11?

— Why did Larry Silverstein, leaseholder of the entire WTC collapse say on PBS: "I remember getting a call from the, er, fire department commander, telling me that they were not sure they were gonna be able to contain the fire, and I said, 'We've had such terrible loss of life, maybe the smartest thing to do is pull it.' And they made that decision to pull and we watched the building collapse." ?

— Why did the 9/11 Commission not make any mention of the collapse of WTC 7?

— How could three modern steel skyscrapers defy the laws of physics by collapsing at near free-fall speed through dozens and dozens of undamaged levels?

— What sliced the huge vertical support steel columns into 30' segments, convenient for trucking away?

— Why did all the collapses exhibit every characteristic of controlled demolition, including sudden onset, completely vertical fall, nearly free-fall speed, total collapse, sliced steel, pulverization of concrete and other materials, dust clouds, horizontal ejections, sounds of explosions, molten steel within and below?

— Why was the steel at Ground Zero carted off as quickly as possible – in violation of state and federal statues concerning removal of material at a crime scene – to be melted down in China and other countries?

— How can we explain all of the eyewitness and first-responder testimony of explosions preceding the collapses of the twin towers, or police clearing the WTC 7 area of bystanders because the building "would be coming down"?

THE PENTAGON AND FLIGHT 77

— Why does a 757 smashing into the Pentagon at first floor level make only an 18' hole, and break no windows where the wings and tail should have hit?

— Why is the grass on the Pentagon lawn unscathed when the low-slung 757 engines would have burned or dug it up?

— Why has the FBI confiscated the videos from various private and state security cameras around the Pentagon that can be expected to show the crash of Flight 77, and why will it not release these videos?

— If Flight 77 was "vaporized" in the intense fire following the crash, how did it punch into and out of three rings of the Pentagon, leaving a neat round hole in the final exit hole?

— How can jet engine fuel "vaporize" the very engines that burn it?

— If flight 77 was "vaporized", how did examiners positively identify the remains of all the passengers, and how explain the unburned wood and paper in rooms immediately adjacent?

— After punching through the final exit hole in the "C-ring" of the Pentagon, why did Flight 77, unlike any airline crash in history, leave no wreckage?

THE FLIGHTS - IN GENERAL

— Why were our air defenses unable to intercept any of the hijacked airliners on 9/11, for up to nearly two hours after the first reported hijacking, when wayward aircraft are routinely intercepted?

— How did the FBI come up with a complete list of names and photographs of the alleged 19 hijackers within two days?

— Why are none of the alleged hijackers listed on any of the airlines' passenger manifests or the autopsy reports?

ACTIONS BY THE ADMINISTRATION

— Why did the Bush Administration actively resist the formation of the 9/11 Commission for 441 days, when similar investigations, such as those for Pearl Harbor, the JFK assassination, and the space shuttle disasters, all started in about one week?

— What is the meaning of Secretary of Transportation Norman Mineta's following testimony to the 9/11 Commission about what he observed in the Presidential Emergency Operations Center on the morning of 9/11: "There was a young man who had come in and said to the vice president, "The plane is 50 miles out. The plane is 30 miles out." And when it got down to, "The plane is 10 miles out, "the young man also said to the vice president, "Do the orders still stand?" And the vice president turned and whipped his neck around and said, "Of course the orders still stand. Have you heard anything to the contrary?" If the orders were to shoot the plane down, why wasn't it shot down? An explanation for the young man's continued, perplexed questioning might be that the orders were for the plane NOT to be shot down. Why did the 9/11 Commission not mention this testimony in its final report?

— Why did Bush and Cheney agree to speak with the 9/11 Commission only on the conditions that 1) they do so in each other's company, 2) they not be put under oath, 3) their testimony not be recorded?

— Why were no immediate steps taken to remove President Bush and his entourage from the elementary school in Sarasota after it was learned that the second tower had been struck, thus placing the students, as well as the president, at risk?

THE 9/11 COMMISSION

— Why have some 9/11 Commission members said they were lied to by the Pentagon and that the 9/11 Commission was a White House cover-up?

— How can the 9/11 Commission Report be considered authoritative when its members were picked by the president, when its director, Philip Zelikow, an administration intimate, determined what investigations would be made, what witnesses would be heard, and what would go into the final report, and when no members of the Commission were scientists, engineers, or intelligence experts?

WAKE UP, KANSANS! Is this the kind of nation you want to be banded to? One where the possibility – or even the likelihood — of government complicity in the events of 9/11 exists?

A large research community has developed to look seriously into the unanswered questions of 9/11. Go online for the disturbing architectural and engineering reports, photos, videos — all ignored by the mass media. Google such sites as:

= Journal of 911 Studies
= 9/11 Truth
= Physics 911
= What Really Happened
= Architects and Engineers for 9/11 Truth
= Pilots for 9/11 Truth
= 911 Blogger
= Reopen 911
= 911 Research WTC 7

Read their material and follow their links if you dare: Then contact us at P.O Box 3461, Liberal, KS 67901, email us at freekansas@yahoo.com, or visit our website at www.freekansas.org

COMMUNIQUÉ number 2

TWENTY-SEVEN

And the Fourth Beast Was Like a Flying Eagle

Frustration, yes. But concerning the great Event itself, all was almost there. The last tasks were poised to be accomplished: for Miles, preparing the building; for Gronsky & Skulk, learning to fly a Cessna.

The former was accomplished via Miles' connections, apparent experience, and with the unintended cooperation of the Children's Miracle Network, a non-profit organization dedicated to saving and improving the lives of children by raising funds for children's hospitals.

You know those little angel medallions you see plastered all over supermarket windows, inscribed in crayon with dollar-donors' names,? In the month of November, these began to appear on the structural pillars of Kaufmann's Department store, covering over quarter-inch holes, laser-drilled nightly, now loaded with state-of-the-art plastique tamped and retouched with expertly-matched paint.

Who would doubt the legitimacy of this program? Who would dare to lift the angels' skirts to see what might lie under them? What janitor, what manager even, would do anything but warmly smile, pleased as Punch by Kansan generosity?

If the theory of Miles's work was simple, the application was complex. Using five grams of high explosive in each of 400 holes on first, fifth, ninth and twelfth floors columns — only enough explosive to eliminate critical structural support — the center section of the roof should drop, pulling the rest of the structure in and down. Detached from their moorings, beams once braced by a column would turn into unstable cantilevers, rotating earthward, pulling the walls inward when loaded from above — and the building would collapse under its own weight. The placement of charges is crucial, as is the linked timing of detonations — upward, downward, inward, outward — with their pre-determined delays. Many hours of computer time went into the planning, and it was angelic beings which hid, and marked, the details. "Just like downtown," Miles thought.

Throughout December, seraphim and cherubim metastasized along key columns, and had any mischievous breeze Marilyn-Monroe'd a skirt, an acute observer might have glimpsed — if the light were right — two tiny contacts for the blasting caps, like spider fangs, glinting through the paint. But Kaufmann's was centrally heated, so breezes there were none. The scheme seemed to be working.

In the daytime, Miles's day-job: Columbus Discovering Wichita; The Wicked Witch of the East, and her (puppet) Cat, Tige; in November, Guy Fawkes who, in 1605 tried to blow up the British Parliament with 36 barrels of gunpowder, was executed, and is remembered by some as "the only man ever to enter Parliament with honest intentions" — Mile's favorite fact learned at Yale.

> *Remember, remember, the 5th of November,*
> sang out the tape loop,
> *Gunpowder, treason and plot.*
> *So check out our sportswear for hunting and horsewear*
> *You'll find that our prices are hot!*

In later November, there were a variety of Pilgrims and Indians, played variously; in December, Santa Bubbie for Hanukkah. And Miles was now preparing for his final, hallmark role as St. Nicholas.

But nights — late nights — Miles played in that other show, a two-man show, actually, one active, one passive, the latter his strange, bearded confederate, a night watchman called Isaac Smith, he of the glowing eyes — whose only role was to turn those eyes away from the action, and then to take an extended, out-of-the-building break early on Christmas morning. But Isaac watched without eyes, and occasionally commented aloud in the dark, empty, otherwise quiet store, with a favorite Sacred Harp tune.

The day is past and gone
The evening shades appear,
O may we all remember well
The night of death is near.

We lay our garments by
Upon our beds to rest [this, in bedroom furniture]
So death will soon disrobe us all

Of what we here possess.
Lord keep us safe this night
Secure from all our fears
May angels guard us while we sleep [while fondling the last-night's-posted hosts]
Till morning light appears.

All thoughts appropriate for an ancient night-watchman with much to reflect on.

Meanwhile back at Gronsky & Skulk's, aeronautics proceeded apace. Miles had presented the team with flight training software, a joystick (which Skulk thought should refer to something else), and a third-party accessory belt — though accessory to what they had yet to discover.

The flight trainer came from Sadosoft, a division of Terminal Reality Software. The name was strange enough, but stranger was its "Read Me First", a message from the developer, Arturo Indelicado:

> **Thank you for using Sadosoft Fly!**
> **First the bad news.**
> Without special intervention, we are ineligible for Heaven. This applies to the entire human race. You are not alone. No good works you can do will save you from being eternally damned.
> **But there is good news!**
> There is a simple and free way to be reconciled with God, made possible by God's only son. Placing your complete trust in Jesus' death, burial

and resurrection is God's one and only permitted means of reaching Heaven. This is a free gift from God because He loves you.

Manufacturer's Warning:
Sadosoft Fly! is not for real-world flying. Using it for purposes other than entertainment is at your own risk. Flight training is a lot like toilet training: it can be somewhat dangerous.

Our motto:
"Truth or Consequences."

Miles had warned them about Arturo, a known crackpot, but the acknowledged genius of the flight-simulation field. They were not to mind his popup messages relating technique issues to biblical verse and commentary. Arturo, Miles said, was lonesome, and had too much time on his hands. "Attached to his workstation at Sadosoft," Miles told them, "the man has a quote from Henry James: 'Art derives a considerable part of its beneficial exercise from flying in the face of presumptions.' So trust me," Miles assured them, "Just concentrate on the task at hand, and let Arturo take you there."

Yes. Well.

Indelicado's breakthrough in training pedagogy was to incorporate "failure-modeling" right from the start. The idea, Miles explained, was well understood. Like pigeons on an electric grid, pecking at buttons for food, or *Planaria* flatworms in an electrified Y-maze learning the difference between go-left and go-right, humans can also be trained — quickly and well — by administering disagreeable consequences to maladaptive behavior. In other words, if mistakes are no big deal, they continue to be made. But in an airplane, they can be fatal. Best not to make them. And so, "truth or consequences."

Sadosoft's consequences ranged from the attention-grabbing silly (large virtual chickens pecking at your hands from inside the screen) to the quite serious (crash the plane — crash your computer; crash with potentially fatal consequences — hard-drive data destroyed, amounts increasing with each repetition; crash with destruction of landlubbers or their property — drive destruction and potential hardware fire). An eye for an eye (Ex 21:23-5) or worse — one of life's fundamental principles. It was surprising how quickly people thus tutored could learn.

On the other hand, Indelicado, like YHWH, understood that people have to be given the chance to <u>make</u> mistakes if they were to learn from making them. And even be tempted to do so.

And so, moving his cursor over the prominent "Quick Start" icon, Richard, the alpha-male of Gronsky & Skulk, found the "Option for novices who want to jump right into the pilot's chair, or veterans who just want a quick flight fix." Sure, let's give it a try. What human with only one X chromosome could resist?

And there he was, in full-screen mode, inside the cockpit. The propeller started up, the screen began to shake. Gronsky had to turn down the speaker volume when Skulk complained of the engine roar. Wait a minute, the plane was taxiing all by itself out onto the runway; he assumed it would hold at one end while he figured out what to do next. But no! The Cessna began to move forward, picking up speed along the high-detail path, and before the runway's end, lifted off into the sky over an eerily accurate Wichita. "OK, Champ, it's all yours," flashed the screen, to which a bedroomy voice-over added, "Take me for a ride."

The controls were in front of him, but he didn't know what to do. What the hell were all those dials and levers and wheels and pedals? Damn it, I knew I should have read the manual! He started to flail around, using the mouse to push or pull wherever pushing or pulling might have some effect. Do I right click? Hit alt? Or control? Maybe the arrow keys. And the plane careened around, skirting trees and silos, getting dangerously close to downtown. The horizon came and went, and horizontal was terrifyingly elusive and disorienting. This was just a game, but never had he felt so out of control. Thirty seconds felt like an eternity, and when he crashed into a cornfield, he actually felt relieved. The screen exploded and went black. Then, a status report in crackly voice: "The Eagle has landed." And an on-screen announcement:

> **CONGRATULATIONS!**
> **You are dead.**
> **But — you have won the Francis Galton Award for Cleansing the Shallow End of the Gene Pool.**
> **The fewer pilots like you there are,**
> **the safer we'll all be.**
> **In thirty seconds, your computer will crash,**
> **and some of your important data will be lost.**
> **There is nothing you can do to stop this.**
> **Go get it fixed, and don't do it again.**

An exacting teacher was Indelicado. But effective. During repair, Gronsky and Skulk studied every page of the flight manual.

Well, not <u>every</u> page, Miles advised them. For there was much they didn't have to know. Like how to land, for instance. Or how to use the radios, or read half of the controls. They had to know only

— how to start up
— how to taxi
— how to take off
— how to reach 500 feet
— how to turn
— how to aim the plane and fix the trim to hold it on course

and that was it. The rest they already knew — how to do a static-line escape jump, hopefully into Herman Hill Park. The Cessna and he would do the rest.

Still, there were mistakes to be made, and the situation allowed no room for error. Therefore, the belt.

The belt had been developed by DARPA for special forces training, and was now manufactured commercially by VirTra Systems, of Arlington, Texas, the world's leading developer of the Virtual Immersive Reality devices used by domestic and international law enforcement agencies, General Motors, Red Baron Pizza, and the U.S. Air Force. It hadn't come cheap, but the costs were absorbed by an unnamed contact of Miles's. It looked a lot like a weightlifter's belt, thick leather with a broad area against the small of the back, but connected, too, to a heavy shoulder strap which passed over the right chest. A power cord went to a transformer, and thence to the wall, and a USB connection was made from computer to belt to prompt it. The rheostat was situated out of the student's easy reach.

Using the belt took some heavy convincing. Normal flight training assumed a cushion of time and space which Gronsky & Skulk would not have, Miles argued. If they were to make a mistake at twelve or fifteen thousand feet, they would have plenty of time to think, and to correct: Messrs. Bernoulli and Cessna would be there to hold them up. Not so at five hundred feet, a quarter mile from target. Under those conditions, even small errors — the kind which might call forth only the Indelicadian chickens — that level of error could be fatal — to them, or to the mission. No time, no space for rectification. The level of tolerance had to be zero. That was the purpose of the belt.

No problem, Miles assured them. They could adjust the voltage to comfortable discomfort — just enough to keep their pulse rate up, and their adrenalin high. Lots of oxygen to the brain, lots of adrenergic stimulation yielded fewer errors, faster, deeper training, more successful results. Pavlov knew what he was about.

Though Gronsky got used to it, and even enjoyed it — somewhat, Skulk always felt violated, electrically raped by an invisible admirer as erratic and demanding as her fraternity swains. She wasn't into bondage. Still, she submitted, as much for the macho, as for her dedication to The Event. By mid-December, both Gronsky & Skulk were Cessna experts — at least for the ascending part of the flight, sans radio. There hadn't been a chicken attack on either of them in hundreds of flight-hours logged, even while confronting Indelicado's most demonic "random" failures.

They felt ready to go.

TWENTY-EIGHT

The Last Interview

'Twas the night before Christmas, and Gronsky & Skulk were meditating on the morrow. The stockings were hung, not by the chimney, which the apartment didn't have, but, laden with pomegranates and oranges, were loading down the middle branches of a tree from Home Depot. There were presents, too, below, all saved for after The Event.

A little before eight, there was a clattering on the hallway stairs, and a pounding at the door. Carolers from the WSU Early Music Society? No. It was J.B. Libby in a Santa hat, come all the way from Cullison, standing there with a cheery, beribboned present, a sheet metal sculpture of the Twin Towers, papered with stock columns from the Wall Street Journal.

"Here," he said, with alcohol on his breath. "I brought this for you. No one else in town wanted it."

"Thank you, thank you so much," Skulk said, beckoning him in like the gracious hostess she was trained to be.

"But how did you find us?" Gronsky asked.

"You think all us geezer hicks are dumb? You got a name? I looked you up."

"You remembered our names. How nice," Skulk cried with pleasure.

"Bonnie Ann wrote 'em down. She writes down all our visitors."

"So did you just come to give us this present?" Richard asked. "It's terrific. So true, so true... "

"No." He walked across the room, and sat down at the kitchen table. "I came to gripe and get you to do something about it." He directed his talk to Gronsky. "You're the only one I know, you and Tom Frank, and he don't answer me — he must think I want to sue him or something — who knows these guys."

"What guys?"

Libby pulled a tattered newspaper article out of his coat pocket.

"Well, like this guy Foner — he's a history professor, right? Like you."

Richard nodded. "Eric. Yes. At Columbia."

"Yeah. Him. And the director of the ACLU, Romero, and this Jewish human rights guy, Posner. 'Stop Torture Now". Tom Bernstein... you know them, right?"

"I have met some of them — but just at conferences. I wouldn't say I know them really. What about them?"

"Have you heard about the plans for the 9/11 memorial?"

"Not much," Skulk answered for both of them.

"You should take all this down on your tape recorder, ma'am. Add it to my interview, ok?"

"Sure," she said, and went to her desk to get the machine. Libby waited till it was on to speak further.

"So you know they're planning this International Freedom Center for a 9/11 memorial — right there at ground zero, right over the bodies of the people that were killed, and the people who tried to rescue them. It's an affront... "

"Who is planning it?" Richard asked.

"Foner and Romero and Posner, Bernstein — the liberals."

"Why is it an affront?"

"Well, ma'am you obviously don't know what's in it."

"Tell me," Skulk said.

"It's this whole Blame America First, like we <u>deserved</u> to be attacked. A big exhibit about Abu Whateveryoucallit, blowing the whole thing out of proportion — as if murdering thousands of innocent Americans was nothing compared to a couple of bad apples putting underwear on the heads of these guys out to kill us. Here, listen... "

He ran along the small print with his still-mittened hand.

"'... a high tech, multimedia tutorial about man's inhumanity to man, from Native American genocide to the lynchings and cross-burnings of the south, from the Third Reich's Final Solution to the Soviet gulags and beyond... ' You think that kind of shit is appropriate? Right over the ashes of Ground Zero? What about the atrocity, and how ordinary Americans became heroes, and how we all came together to fight back? Shit, no, that's not what gets a memorial. That's not politically correct. Instead of remembering the dead, we get a lesson from liberals about how we deserve to die because we're Americans."

"I don't think that's what they're saying... " Gronsky began.

"You said you didn't know beans about it!"

"He means that one doesn't take away from the other," Skulk explained.

"Listen, these plans have just come out. They've been kept secret all this time. Why is that? Like we should grant prisoners at Gitmo all the legal rights of the Americans they murdered?"

"The prisoners at Guantanamo weren't involved in the attacks."

"Yeah, they were — in Afghanistan. Trying to kill our boys."

"So what would you like me to do about this?" Richard asked, seeing that any rational argument was futile, and wanting to go back to quiet-space asap in preparation for the morning.

"I want you to call up your buddies... "

"They're not... "

"OK, your friends, your acquaintances. And George Soros — he's who's funding this. You can call them easier than I can. And I want you to explain what I said to them — cause they sure as hell won't listen to me. And I want you to get this bullshit stopped. (Fist on the table.) We can't be attacking the morale of our troops when they're out there in harm's way, fighting for us."

The room was quiet.

"You got that down?" Libby asked.

"Skulk nodded.

"Lemme hear. Play back a little."

"*... morale of our troops when they're out there in harm's way fighting for us.*"

"Good. So you'll play that for them? Your friends? And put in a word?"

"I will," said Gronsky. "And we'll also be sure to put it in the book."

"You want this article?" He held out the crumpled clipping.

"No, no," Gronsky responded. "You take it. I can google the information."

"What's google?"

"A way to look things up. On the computer."

"Oh. Bonnie Ann does all that stuff. I got <u>real</u> work to do. OK, gotta go. Long drive back. You like your Christmas present?"

"Oh, yes. It's fabulous. We'll put it in a place of honor — here, right on top of this bookshelf."

"See?" Richard added, "right next to *The Federalist Papers.*"

"What's them?"

"Oh, you know, the stuff written by Hamilton and Madison to… "

"The Founding Fathers?"

"Founding as you can get."

"Good enough for me, then."

He shook their hands heartily, and wobbled off down the stairs.

"Be sure you put that in the book," he called back up.

"We will," they yelled down. "Good night. Drive safely."

They resumed their meditation with brows more furrowed than before.

TWENTY-NINE

Windhovers

Brute beauty and valour and act, oh, air, pride, plume, here Buckle!
Gerard Manley Hopkins

The night had been still and starry, and the day promised to be as clear as its prototype, 9/11/2001. And a good thing, too, since neither pilot was well-equipped to handle weather, nor would any tower keep them grounded.

Miles had called at five to rouse them — as if they'd been asleep — and to give them the good news: a 1984 Cessna 172, the old warhorse of a sky-diving school in Nebraska, was on the ground at the plant, waiting for an upgrade to its instrument panel. That would be their chariot, and better to waste a $10,000 plane than a $100,000 one. It would die a noble death.

The sky was coming slowly awake, brightening to pale orangey-pink as the three drove southwest through a deserted city, over the river to Cessna Drive. And there, at its terminus, was the landing strip of the historic Cessna plant, the enterprise that had turned Wichita into "The Aviation City". They parked on the street, and walked to the gate, Miles in parka, jeans and Santa hat, and the pilots in insulated jumpsuits and helmets, well-strapped into their parachute packs.

There to meet them was the third-shift watchman, Shabel Morgan, a bearded ancient with Old Testament eyes. He nodded to them silently, unlocked the gate, and led them to the Skyhawk. It was already fueled up — to 3 gallons left and right — enough to get them to target, but not enough to create the size fire that might serve as explanation for a building's collapse. After checking out the rig and synchronizing watches, Miles gave the final briefing. The Event would occur by 7 AM at the latest. The videocams had been set up and were already rolling. He would alert the *Eagle* to their press conference when he saw both canopies open, and the building would be pulled after they had both safely hit the ground. He left for his post at the detonator.

Gronsky & Skulk climbed into the aircraft. Shabel handed them the key. They began their shortened pre-flight check.

But wait. What the hell. Nothing was as in the book. The instruments were all higgledy-piggledy on the dash. Where were "the sacred six", conveniently grouped? They located the ASI, the attitude gyro, the altimeter, the turn coordinator, the gyrocompass and the VSI scattered over the dash. They found the tachometer, and the temp and pressure and fuel gauges. The throttle and mixture knobs were where they should be, and the trim controls pedals and yoke were as they had been trained for. There were only two radios and not a stack, but they wouldn't be using them. The lights were also irrelevant.

But in spite of their initial disorientation, this old skydiving 182 was an excellent choice. It was a four-seater, whose all-but-the-pilot seats had been removed, giving them far more room to maneuver. The normal passenger door had been replaced by a large flap hinged at the top for easier escape, with a vise-grip as the makeshift handle. The interior seemed held together by geological strata of duct-tape, and most inventive of all, outside, over the wheel, a tiny platform had been built so that the jumper could grab the strut and stand alongside the plane to orient before casting off. Yes, this would be their Grane, and a good old Grane she was!

Gronsky was at the controls. He turned on the engine, and they completed their pre-flight check: controls, instruments, gas, attitude, runup, safety — and gave a thumbs up to Miles's grizzled friend outside. Shabel gave them the classic ground-control "go" sign, and pointed them out to the runway. On this windless early morning, they headed east northeast, directly towards the city.

Shabel waved them goodbye, and sang them, unheard, a bon voyage:

*And when we early rise
And view th'unwearied sun
May we set out to win the prize
And after glory run.*

He trudged back to the office, his breath steaming the air as he sung *sotto voce*:

*And when our days are past and gone
And we from time remove
O may we in thy bosom rest
The bosom of thy love.*

Gronsky brought Grane to an efficient climb speed, and at 1,500 feet, as planned, trimmed to straight-and-level flight. The Kaufmann building was ahead and to their right. As he passed it, he banked the plane into a long 280-degree right turn, which would bring them facing north, about four miles from the target, where he leveled off, heading directly toward the building. He adjusted speed to bring the nose down, and trimmed to an attitude which would intersect with the building's top floors. Just south of their mark, the river made a turn to the east, and the park lay directly under their approach.

Skulk opened the door flap. The plane pulled unexpectedly to the right from the increased resistance. Still at the controls, Richard compensated. Skulk lowered her goggles, climbed out on the wheel, and clung to the strut.

"Say when," she yelled.

Gronsky unbuckled, climbed out of his seat, and keeping an eye on the target, he situated himself on the passenger side, for exit as soon as Skulk had jumped. Even from 500 feet, they thought, they could each control canopy enough to come down close to one another within ten seconds.

"Ready?" he shouted.

"Yes," she yelled back.

"Go!"

It takes approximately 6 seconds for a stone to fall 500 feet. For a woman with a quickly opening 35' parachute, make that 20. Not a lot of time to look around, or think things through. She didn't see Gronsky's canopy above her, but she figured he must simply be behind her angle of vision. She landed hard, as Miles had expected, but did a staged roll, as she had been taught, to absorb the impact. Feet, calf, thighs, butt, small of back: it worked.

Recovering, she looked around for her partner, and saw the plane, its nose embedded in the building a few blocks to the north. But where was he? Was she alone? Where was the ampersand? There had to be an ampersand!

Just then, a huge explosion, and she saw the top floor of Kaufmann's Department Store fall directly into the one below it, and then another explosion, and another, and another, and the building fell earthward at close to free-fall speed, collapsing neatly into itself, just as she'd seen Building 7 do so many times on videos. That Miles, she thought. What good work. What fine, accomplished work.

But where was Richard? <u>Where was Richard?</u> She looked desperately around, and saw behind her two men running in her direction. One tackled her to the ground; the other slipped a black hood over her head. She felt her harness being cut from her body.

She screamed at them, but there was no answer from her attackers. She beat at them as she could, but they pinned her arms, cuffed them behind her, carried her, sack-wise, to a car, and shoved her in the back.

THIRTY

All the News That's Fit to Print

The special evening edition of the Wichita Eagle ran a front-page string of time-lapsed stills, and a 72 point headline: CHRISTMAS TRAGEDY, with the subhead Two-Timed Husband Takes Life, Sends Love. The website featured a 3-minute video of the plane crash, and the building's collapse. The story over the fold ran as follows:

"This will be my final landing," the pilot radioed the control tower. "Please call my wife at 316-[number withheld], and tell her I love her, I still love her. I'll always love her. Tell her I'll always love her. Over and out. Out, out, out."

And with that, Thomas Torpy, 43, changed his transponder squawk to 7700, the emergency code, and flew his Cessna 152 straight into the 12th story of Kaufmann's Department Store, on Broadway and Mt. Vernon, wrecking the plane, killing himself, and setting the building ablaze.

Minutes later, the ancient building, unable to withstand such stress or fire, collapsed, as its uninsulated steel beams buckled from the intense heat.

Mercifully, no one was in the building so early on Christmas morning — a gift, perhaps, from the Spirit of Christmas itself.

Go to www.wichitaeagle.com/airplane to see the video.

Within two days, the site had gotten 130,700 hits.

Within two months, all but the image of the plane, its wings sheared off, its fuselage and tail protruding 12 stories over Mt. Vernon Avenue, had been forgotten too — as America moved on.

AFTERWORD

Afterword:
Fighting Fiction with Fiction

After seven years, the resistance to 9/11 truth studies continues to astound. Many very smart people, lefties, political activists - people who don't believe one word of what anyone in the Bush administration says – for some reason believe every word of the preposterous official version of 9/11. Unlike any other blather from Washington, this seems to be the story they want to believe. In any case, when I've tried to raise the subject, they will "not go there". "Not going there" always involves the same hand gestures – both arms raised from the elbows, palms out, slightly in front of the face, blocking passage to the ears.

What's going on? It's not as if these people have no political analysis, or hold worldviews which won't tolerate 9/11 truth investigation. A standard explanation is that some truths are so destructive the most common defense is total denial. When I tried to bring up the subject, one woman actually said to me, "I don't want to live in a world where such things could happen." Well, if openness to thinking about 9/11 necessitates suicide, I can understand her reaction.

But there are many kinds of suicide. In my case, there is the suicide envisioned for me as an author by publishers, and a possible secondary suicide of their publishing houses for associating themselves with an author who might be perceived as a tin-hatted conspiracy wacko. In the case of normal, mainstream, journalism, it seems again to be the editor protecting the writer from suicide, and, more importantly, keeping the publication safe from assault - - as the owners protect the public from the need to think. In any case, fiction or nonfiction which explores alternative stories and explanations of 9/11 seems to be firmly censored in the womb with little protest from the pro-life crowd.

I first started thinking about 9/11 fiction after writing an early review of David Ray Griffin's first book, The New Pearl Harbor. http://counterpunch.org/estrin05252004.html. In 2004, there were still so many unanswered questions and so little evidence with which to construct answers. As in any investigation, the first step is speculation: who might have done it, how might it have happened? Forensic investigation is well left to experts, but speculation itself is often best done by creative writers. So while Griffin and other investigators pursued their work, why not ask my fellow fiction writers to think about some clues?

I put out a call to the small circle of writers I happen to know, angling for 9/11 short stories for a possible anthology. I was surprised to see so few come in, and of those few there were even fewer that, qualitywise, were likely to be publishable. So I abandoned the anthology project, and thought, "I'll just do it myself." Out came this novel, *Skulk*.

Skulk was a pleasure to write. It was fun actually having <u>fun</u> writing about 9/11! And I thought such a book might actually make an end run around the censorship on the topic.

I submitted it enthusiastically for publication and submitted it again, and again: no one would touch it except for John Leonard at Progressive Press (kindly suggested by Webster Tarpley). John hadn't published much fiction before, at least not intentionally, but decided to give this a try.

There remains the question of how to reach beyond the initiates who are already looking for the kind of books Progressive Press put out. This is a general problem beyond that of 9/11 truth fiction. As activists, we all have to find ways to reach beyond the choir. What about 9/11 truth? As Dick Cheney so pithily observed, "So?" So the government is tricking the people? What's new? So the American government has murdered its own citizens in pursuit of its goal of world domination? "I don't have a dog in that fight."

Fighting Fiction with Fiction

As my publisher, John Leonard, sees it,

It's the old problem of the Big Lie. They got plausible deniability by doing something so unbelievably outrageous that it really can't be believed by most people. A lot of us who could see through it hitched our wagon to 9/11, figuring that it was dynamite, the highest-powered door-opener around. After seven years, it looks like it's no silver bullet after all. We might have to start a bit further back with people -- maybe all the way back with learning how conditioning works? I'm reprinting one classic on that subject, but mainly I'm branching out from 9/11 and trying to cover the whole conspiracy, bit by bit, to build up people's background information. Marc Estrin's approach is a very creative one on these lines -- to look for side doors that may be open, instead of trying to drive another truck through the front gate. Maybe that's why he called it 'Skulk' -- it's a stealth approach to 9/11 Truth."

The problem seems to be that so many of us – most of us – are "embedded." We are embedded in a culture whose frame has expanded to include anything that happens. There is no longer anything "beyond the pale." Everything is normal, bipartisan, omnipartisan, cloaked in the magic power of "whatever."

I had thought that the <u>one</u> thing that the American public would not put up with would be the idea that its own government had attacked it on 9/11. That's still probably the case. But between that truth and its consequences stands The Great Wall of Denial. It seems one cannot simply argue people over the wall, or hand them a factual triptik to get there. So in *Skulk* I have tried another strategy: the characters simply believe in 9/11 truth, so they are incorporated, not debated, into the underlying structure of the novel. As would-be activists, Gronsky & Skulk, pursue their goal – our goal – of public enlightenment, they are totally frustrated. But the websites they publish in their Calls to the People are real. Any reader who decides to check them – as many readers will now do, having grown used to hyperlinks -- will find him or herself bathing in the wealth of facts and ideas that real 9/11 researchers have come up. In this way, I hope to have brought the

9/11 material to a new cohort — that of readers of (comic) fiction who might not otherwise come in contact with them.

Since September 13, 2001, I have been standing every weekday from 5-5:30 at a busy Burlington intersection with a group of vigilers, each with his or her own sign, protesting the many things there are to protest. I have thought it best to use my own signs to simply inject an idea into public discourse. For several years before the word became common, my sign simply said IMPEACH. Impeach who? That was up to the viewer. Once the word "impeachment" became common in public discussion, I changed my sign to read "GOT FASCISM?", a concept we are not yet commonly talking about. I often get questions from passersby — "what is that — fascism?" Sometime the pronunciation is comical. It amazes me, but there are many people who have forgotten — or never knew.

In the same way, I would like *Skulk* to simply put the materials of the 9/11 truth movement into circulation for the fiction-reading crowd. *Skulk* does not argue, it does not prove, it assumes the reader knows all about it. And on some level, I believe that many denying Americans do know. It needs only to be brought into legitimate discussion. 9/11 fiction may be another, possibly successful, doorway to that discussion.

ABOUT THE AUTHOR

Marc Estrin is a writer, cellist and activist from Burlington, Vermont, and author of the novels
Insect Dreams, The Half Life of Gregor Samsa (2002);
The Education of Arnold Hitler (2005);
Golem Song (2006);
The Lamentations of Julius Marantz (2007);
The Annotated Nose (2008);
and an award-winning memoir of his decades-long work with the Bread & Puppet Theater,
Rehearsing With Gods: Photographs and Essays on the Bread & Puppet Theater (with Ron Simon, photographer) (2004)

More information may be found on his website, http://web.mac.com/mestrin .

Lightning Source UK Ltd.
Milton Keynes UK
UKOW050924050713

213274UK00001B/17/P